FURORE

N.J. ADEL

FURORE

This is a work of fiction. All incidents and dialogue, and all characters are products of the author's imagination. Any resemblance to persons living or dead, similar books or characters is entirely coincidental.

Copyright © 2022 N.J. Adel
All rights reserved.
ISBN: 9798808633469
Salacious Queen Publishing

DEDICATION

To tattoos and Adonis belts
You make us dumb as fuck
But you're totally worth it

ALSO BY N.J. ADEL

Contemporary Romance
The Italian Heartthrob
The Italian Happy Ever After
The Italian Marriage
The Italian Obsession
The Italian Dom
The Italian Son

Paranormal Reverse Harem
All the Teacher's Pet Beasts
All the Teacher's Little Belles
All the Teacher's Bad Boys
All the Teacher's Prisoners

Reverse Harem Erotic Romance
Her Royal Harem: Complete Box Set

Dark MC and Mafia Romance
Furore
Tirone
Dusty
Cameron

TABLE OF CONTENTS

FURORE

CHAPTER 1

JO

His eyes reminded me of my worst and most beautiful mistake.

They made me as nervous as I was on the first afternoon I drove to teach here. Questions, self-doubt and self-preservation had kicked in. A men's prison classroom wasn't exactly the best or the safest place for a twenty-three-year-old female teacher to be. Would the *students* see a teacher or prey? Would they respect me? Would they listen to what my mind had to offer or would I be reduced to a body, a form of entertainment, a fantasy to warm up their lonely nights?

After a couple of classes, I'd stopped asking those questions because, much to my surprise, many students here had been more engaged and curious about Creative Writing than I'd seen in a regular high school class. The inmates really wanted to learn. Aside from all the trivial stuff like gates, visitor forms, the occasional catcalls and uncooperative guards…and the terrible smell, I never regretted volunteering here. I loved coming to San Quentin State Prison every week. The Arena as the inmates called it. It was my way to make amends, to atone. If I'd ever be redeemed.

Until Laius Lazzarini joined my class.

Even though he hardly spoke, the intense way he looked at me—which felt an awful lot like the look that had brought me to my knees and made me do the unpredictable—sent back the anxiety…and the memory.

As if it's ever left me…

The summer was half gone, and I was still haunted by the eyes that had abandoned me, the dark green pools that would hold me captive and make me submit to whatever they demanded. An exaggeration? Not unlikely. An act of sheer stupidity? Absolutely. No clever woman would have ever made the choices I'd made.

No matter what I did, though, I couldn't get Tirone Wisely's eyes off my mind, missing the way they made my mouth dry yet other parts of me wet, that I was searching for them even in the worst of places...like in the face of a convicted criminal.

It was pure agony, the reminder, but behind the sunglasses I pretended to forget on my face every class, I wouldn't stop taking those gazes back at Laius. Couldn't.

It wasn't only because the president of the Night Skulls MC had incredible dark green eyes with an exceptional shade of gray surrounding them that made anything else in their proximity not worth looking at or that the intensity of his stare exuded power, sadness and menace all in one, daring you to look away, knowing you'd fail.

No. I kept staring back because I needed the reminder of my shame, the pain. Deserved it.

"Miss Moonshow, I have a question," one of the students interrupted my awkward staring session, and I didn't need to look to know which one.

Frustration, and a flicker of irritation, pulsed in me as I glanced toward the voice. If

I made the effort to learn how to say Laniakea Kelekolio correctly, why would he not return the courtesy? I'd spent a substantial time on my first class instructing students on how to address me. Knowing that my last name could be a little tricky, I even permitted them to use my first name if they found Miss Meneceo too hard to say. Seriously, how hard could *Miss Jo* be to say or remember? But no, Laniakea Kelekolio found that Miss Moonshow was the most convenient name to call me today.

"It's Meneceo, you idiot," Laius said under his breath and dropped his pencil on the notebook in front of him, tilting his head a little to the side toward Laniakea. "Me-ne-che-yo. How many times is she supposed to say it before you learn it, fucktard?"

My head jerked toward Laius. He'd barely said two words to his classmates since he set foot in my class, not even in greeting, always minding his own business and forcing the others to do the same with his intimidating stares. Having the urge to break his silence— and barriers—to correct my name on another man's tongue sent an unfamiliar, warm, fuzzy feeling through me, as if he'd just defended my honor, not just told someone how to pronounce my last name.

"Not everybody here is fucking Italian, Furore. It took me a while to say yours the way your Italian royal ass likes it," Laniakea said.

Laius rolled his eyes. "Furore is an English word, too, dickhead."

"No, it's not."

"Actually, it is," I intervened. "It means an uproar." Which I found odd to be the road name of a man as quiet as Laius. Maybe he wasn't too quiet outside of those gates. Or maybe he had a reputation of making girls go so loud in a furore...

Or he's just from Furore, Italy, you dirty slut.

"What the..." Laniakea scrunched his nose at me, and then he shook his head at Laius. "Just mind your fucking shit and finish the fucking assignment."

Laius smirked. "Already done."

"Fucking showoff."

"Laniakea, remember what we practiced three classes ago?" I was no longer fazed by the inmates' use of the F word like their lives depended on it whenever they spoke, but if they had to swear, at least, they had to be creative about it. It was one of my first assignments for them. Creative swearing. Everybody seemed to have enjoyed that class in particular, and I still had their papers to prove these men knew how to be creative when they wanted to be.

"Well, sorry, Miss M…Jo." He glared at Laius. "Away, you three-inch fool."

I stifled a gasping laugh, expecting a riot. As the class erupted in sneers, and the guard in the room clutched his baton, I took a step back, reflexively, but my stare never left Laius's face. Harmless joke or not, even the politest of men lost their composure when penis size was involved. Would he snap? It was always the quiet ones you should be most afraid of. He was in for assault with a deadly weapon after all.

But he didn't even blink. With all the confidence and nonchalance in the world, the corner of his mouth curved higher. "Oh, I'll show you how many inches I got for you when I'm deep in your *bone hole*."

Bone hole…I like that.

The class went louder than acceptable. Thankful that their desks and chairs were bolted to the floor or else it'd have been a real, chaotic riot in here, I tapped the surface of my desk twice hard enough to make enough noise to gain their attention. That, along with the guard striding toward me, raising his voice at them in warning, releasing his baton, brought the class under control again.

"All right. From now on, no word sparring in class, please," I said, feeling comfortable to walk around again. "If you feel the urge to swear, nonetheless, don't say it but write it down in your notebook. One single sentence to sum it all up, and to make it challenging enough, no F word allowed. Now back to your assignment. You have exactly four more minutes to finish up."

I went over to Laniakea to let him finally ask his question. Then, on the way back to my desk, I couldn't resist taking a peek at what Laius was writing now in his notebook since he was already done with the assignment.

"Thou art a boil, a plague sore, an embossed carbuncle in my corrupted blood," I read quietly, my skin tingling with every word.

"It's not meant for you, *Miss Meneceo.*"

His voice, low and so very masculine, vibrated through my core. The Italian accent he played with my name had my whole body buzzing. And with every warm breath he let fall on my wrist, an inexplicable throb of my heart hummed over my thoughts. I stood there, in his space, in the heat radiating from his body that was hotter than July's air, speechless for a moment or two, even immobile.

"Art thou well, *Miss Meneceo?*" He let out a chuckle.

My head whipped up as I swallowed. The way he kept saying my name, in that accent, in that…voice… He might be speaking lightly or innocently, but by the smirk I caught on his plump lips, and the darkness of his gaze that was meant to keep everybody else away but, again, trapped me in, it felt intentional. He knew what he was doing, and I should have understood there wasn't an ounce in *Furore* that was innocent.

I cleared my throat, dragging my eyes and myself away. "You read King Lear?"

"Yes, ma'am," he suddenly drawled in a Southern accent.

I'd read in his file he was from Texas. Damn, he really didn't have a single shred of innocence in his two-hundred pounds of tattoo-covered muscles. Christ, how many tattoos did he have? There were skulls and roses all over his sun-kissed arms, the visible part of his skin the chambray shirt allowed and even on his neck…back and front.

"Good for you." Despite everything, I was genuinely impressed. To read one book was something. To read Shakespeare and understand it was something else. To quote from it and use it in proper context was extraordinary in such environment.

"However, I feel you're too advanced for my class. I still wonder why you elected to join us." I'd made all the students write a passage or two about why they joined this class and what they hoped to gain from it on the first day, but Laius hadn't been there yet, and I'd never gotten access to his intentions or goals.

Would he give me some bullshit about reformation and joining college, like most of the students had said, even though he was in his forties? Would he be honest like the very few that blatantly had said it was to help with their parole?

His stare drifted to the bars in the upper side of the wall. The only part of the room that allowed the sunlight in. The orange late afternoon speckles danced on his pupils and gave his dark blond hair the perfect shimmer. God, he was gorgeous. Strangely, I found myself wondering about his safety in a violent place such as prison.

Focus, Jo. He almost killed a man, and he's the president of a notorious motorcycle club. He can take care of himself. Worry about your own safety, girl, because you obviously need it.

"I have my reasons," he finally said.

Ambiguous much? "I'm very much interested in knowing what they are."

His eyes returned to hold me in place. "I prefer not to share, *Miss Meneceo.*"

Son of a… I folded my arms over my chest, cocking a brow to deflect from the annoying throbbing in my heart and between my legs. "Well, you have to. Everybody else did when they first joined. You're no exception."

"And if I respectfully decline?"

I narrowed my gaze at him, even if he couldn't see it. "You will not pass this class."

CHAPTER 2

FURORE

W hen she folded her arms over her chest, I could finally see a hint of the shape of her tits under that ugly suit she chose to wear whenever she came to class. Same style, different bleak colors. As if she'd gone to the most prudish store in San Francisco and bought the same suit in all available colors especially for San Quentin.

Today, the suit was gray. It hid everything her figure was supposed to show. She must have thought this place was full of dangerous monsters that didn't have any pussy in a while, and a fucking suit was shapeless and wouldn't flaunt her curves. At least, that was her logic because who the fuck wore a suit in July?

But in reality, even in that old school principal outfit, the brunette hiding behind those lame ass shades had curves she couldn't hide even if she was wearing a potato sac. I bet every motherfucker in this room had been taking measures in their heads and beating their stinky little meat to them, even the fucking guard. I knew I had.

"You will not pass this class." Her mouth was pressed into a hard line, daring me to defy her. And when she raised a brow, thinking she could play a power game with me, even threatening me, all I could think of was tossing those goddamn shades on the floor, looking her deep in the eyes—which by the way had a bet going what color they were— while my fingers fluttered inside her, and watching what fucking power she would have left to even stand straight and not fall to her knees.

I let my gaze travel lazily down her body and then back up until it crashed with her blushing cheeks. Even though she stood firm, not moving an inch, her skin was too fair to hide how flustered I'd made her feel.

My cock twitched against the denim to that attitude…and that fucking blush. Damn.

As if I'd just undressed her for real and not just with my eyes, she fixed her jacket. "I expect you have that assignment ready by next class." She lifted her chin and sauntered back to her desk, blessing me with the sight of the sexiest curve to an ass I'd ever seen.

Wrapped in pig-sweating rags or not, she was curvy in all the right places, with an ass that would look spectacular with the imprint of my hands all over it. I smirked at that perfect image.

She ignored me, rather didn't dare look at me, for the rest of the lecture, and I went on scribbling in the notebook until time was up. The guard barked for us to leave our pencils and notebooks and prepare to be hauled back to our cells.

As everybody lined up for the door, I headed straight for her. She looked so tiny when she sat behind her desk, and I towered a good ten inches over her and carried, at least, fifty pounds more than what was on her bones.

She cocked that brow again, and I was sure she was glaring at me behind her shades. "Is there a problem, Laius?"

Laius. Nobody called me that anymore. It sounded strange, as if it was some other man's name, one I no longer knew or ever wanted to be. But when it came out of those bare pink lips, I wanted nothing but to be that man she moaned his name while squirming under.

Ignoring the motherfucking hard-on for now, I leaned forward enough to smell her sweet breath but not to get the guard's panties in a twist. "I have a question. Do you think people have the right to keep secrets?"

Her lashes dropped behind the shades, and I didn't miss the quiver of her small fingers. She rose and busied herself with collecting her books and papers and shoving them inside her bag. "I know where this is going. You're still required to finish the assignment and deliver it by next class."

"Without secrets, we're fucked. You of all people should know and respect that."

Her head snapped up at me. "What's that supposed to mean?"

"It's not fair to ask us to pour out our secrets and tell you why we're really here when you won't do the same. Why are *you* here, Miss Meneceo?"

She chuckled. "This is not how it works. This is my class. I decide what's fair and what's not, what to share and what to keep.

Why I do anything isn't any of your business. You're a student. I'm the teacher. Don't ever forget that."

The bitch likes her power play... Fine. Game on. She has no clue what trouble she's just gotten herself in.

She finished packing her stuff. "But to answer the obvious, what your intellectual abilities haven't allowed you to grasp on your own, I'm here to teach. It's my job. That's what people do. Their jobs."

Is she calling me stupid? I snorted. "And I'm studying with you to go to fucking college like a good boy."

"That's—"

"A lie...just like yours."

That fucking brow again. "Excuse me."

"You're not here because it's your job. There's something else."

"Even if you're correct, it's none of your business."

"Let me ask you something simpler then for the sake of *your* intellectual abilities, Miss *Meneceo*? Are you Italian?"

A muscle ticked in her jaw. "It's obvious from the name."

"And you write your first name with a J?"

"Yes," she stressed impatiently.

With a smirk, I leaned a little bit closer, watching the guard approaching in my peripheral vision. "Allora, my dear *Miss Meneceo*, the Italian alphabet has twenty-one letters, but J has never been one of them."

She blanched in a heartbeat, a hitch to her breath.

"Lazzarini, stand straight, and I don't have all day. Gotta go," the guard barked.

I took a blank piece of paper she'd missed from the desk and stretched two fingers at her, the ones I used to get a tight pussy dripping. "A pencil *per favore*."

She obeyed without a word. *Good girl.* As I took the pencil, my fingers touched the side of her knuckle and lingered. The little gasp that escaped her mouth and the heat coming from her skin went straight to my cock. Bare skin to a naked flame, only I wasn't afraid to burn or get burned.

She withdrew her hand quickly as the guard came to the desk and spied what I was writing. "Writing notes outside your notebook isn't allowed, Lazzarini."

I put down the pencil and waved my empty hands at him, moving away already. "Relax, babe. It's just homework." I glanced at her over my shoulder and nodded at the piece of paper as he grabbed my arm to push me outside. "Here's your precious assignment...*Jo*." Puckering my lips slowly, I whispered her name, and fuck me if it didn't taste so sweet. "Ci vediamo," I winked and whistled an old Italian tune on my way out.

CHAPTER 3

JO

My hands twisted in the sheets as sweat dampened my hair. My eyes clenched along with my jaws while my head pressed into the pillows. A sob rose from my throat as my mind trapped me in a never-ending show of the night that had ruined my life fifteen years ago. "Please," I whimpered into the darkness.

Bang!

Breathless, I shot up into a sitting position with a scream. My eyes darted around the pitch-black room, and I allowed myself to let out a breath, slow and deep, and then a few more until I calmed down. I was just a grown ass woman, alone in her quiet apartment, swimming in her sweat because she'd had a nightmare.

Even in my sleep, the world damaged my dreams with fear. I'd woken this way every day for the past seven weeks, and the grief that hit me every time was all too familiar. I turned on the bedside table lamp, but the light didn't take away the pain of missing her…or the guilt of missing him.

For the few months we'd been together, the nightmares were afraid of Tirone. Even when they dared invade our nights, his murmurs would calm me down while his strong arms banished them away.

With a defeated sigh, I staggered to the bathroom. Flinching at the burst of lights, I glanced at my reflection in the mirror and frowned.

The eyes that I'd been hiding behind sunglasses for being too oddly bright to stay inconspicuous weren't bright at all. I traced the dark shadows under them, my pale skin looking dull and lifeless.

I ran my hand through *my* hair—I'd been wearing it for so long that it started to feel as my own. I even slept with it just in case I had an unexpected visitor at night, in case I'd been found, like my mom and I were found fifteen years ago.

Blinking the memory and the tears away, I locked the bathroom door. Then I looked around, making sure no one was watching even when I knew for a fact I was alone, and took off the wig.

The cream blond strands fell from the tie and hung lank and dry past my shoulders. Instantly, my hand touched the place on my skull that had been fractured that night and had never healed right. While it no longer hurt physically, it brought a shower of piercing emotional aches that would never go away.

Bracing against the sink, I evened my breath, willing the pain away. I splashed some water on my face and looked back up in the mirror. Fifteen years in hiding made it hard to recognize myself in my own skin. I wished I could have worn colored contacts and dyed my hair permanently to transform into Jo Meneceo forever. But with my severe dry eye syndrome, contacts weren't an option I could rely on for long. I wore them briefly for identity verification at the prison and sometimes at school when the weather was cold enough to handle the irritation then I took them off the second I could. That stubborn hair wouldn't relax enough to take all the color. No matter what I did, those roots refused to be anything other than that stupid cream blond that, with those eyes, gave me away.

Even my body wouldn't cooperate when I'd tried to shed some pounds to look any different from that chubby, eight-year-old girl that was supposed to die that night with her mom. Wigs and sunglasses had become my last lifeline to hide ever since I lost the only parent that ever cared about me and paid her life for it.

Letting out a heated, silent scream, I yearned for the only face that calmed me down and took the pain away. The one I lay bare before without hiding who I was. "I wish you were here," I whispered, tears falling against my will. "I wish you didn't leave me like that."

It was wrong of me to think or feel that way. No matter how hard I missed or needed him, we were never meant to be together for long. We never stood a chance. I should be happy for him that he left. I shouldn't be angry that he did without a goodbye. I didn't deserve one.

I should never try to reach him again, but logic didn't stop me from grabbing the burner phone I kept on at all times, in case he reached out, and calling his number in the middle of the night. I was desperate.

"It's Tirone. Do your thing. I'll call back when I feel like it…or not." *Beep.*

My skin broke in goosebumps at his voice. Squeezing my eyes in the darkness, I sank back in bed, my mouth open with all the things I wouldn't bring myself to say.

Quickly, I hung up, cursing at myself. It wasn't like he was going to answer. He'd never answered or returned any of my calls in the past seven weeks, and it was so reckless of me to dial his number that late at night.

I buried my face into the pillow, wetting it with my stupid tears. I was exhausted and afraid and heartbroken and alone. No sleep was deep enough to take any of it away or escape the nightmares. Those, along with the horrible emotions that had been piling up my soul, were ingrained in me and would always be part of who I was.

The darkness and grief within me would never be erased. Just like the past. My fate was sealed, and I was only delaying the inevitable. Sooner or later, I'd be found. Someone would spill the beans to the ruthless king, and he would come to finish what he started to protect his blood kingdom. Whether it'd be my bad luck or a mistake I'd made…like that name…

What the fuck was I thinking? How could I have made such a stupid mistake? Why hadn't I researched it or asked any of the Italian kids at school or even Michele?

I thought if I'd had chosen the name by myself and never told anyone about it, it'd have been safer. No one could be tortured into telling what they didn't know. But here I was, thinking I was a fucking genius, coming up with that name, making it officially mine since I moved to California and went to San Francisco for college, living with that name and on my own for five years without a single incident, and bam. It took one tattooed convict with no high school diploma one second to figure out I had a fake ass name and harbored a secret the size of Texas.

Without secrets, we're fucked. You of all people should know and respect that.

Furore's words rang in my ears, and the suspicions I'd been pushing aside all day snuck back in. What did he really mean by that? He couldn't be on to me. He couldn't be on to anything. He wasn't even from around here or anywhere I'd been. I'd read his file. It couldn't be anything but the unlucky coincidence of pushing the buttons of a smartass, Italian inmate. He wanted to rile me up for forcing him to write that assignment. Nothing more, nothing less.

Right?

"Way to go, *Jo*." All those years, cutting ties with the dreadful past, building this fiery, strong-minded persona to keep people at arm's length, hiding my fear and despair behind quick wits and a sharp tongue, getting a degree and a job and an apartment away from New York, away from Chicago, all that hard work, could vanish in a heartbeat all because of one stupid mistake.

Great. Should I start packing already, uproot myself from my new home and find another one? Where to this time? Fucking Alaska?

I dragged my butt out of bed again and went to my desk. Going through my purse, I pulled out Furore's note. His darn assignment I had to accept in its poor condition.

My eyes landed on the four words on the sheet paper. *Per il mio figlio.*

He had to write it in Italian, of course, to prove a point. It wasn't hard to translate, though. *For my son.*

As simple as the words were, they carried a lot of meaning behind them, heavy and deep. My curiosity was over the top. I wanted to know more. Furore's story wasn't about an outlaw who had gotten into a fight, hurt a man and went to prison for it. There was much more to it, and despite my fear, I wanted to know every detail.

Why was he in my class, studying Creative Writing for his son?

Why when the tip of Furore's finger caught the side of my knuckle did a burning jolt of heat shoot deep into the pit of my stomach?

Why did I not reprimand him for touching me in the first place?

Why did I know, if the situation had repeated itself, I still wouldn't have told him to stop?

I shook my head, shoving the piece of paper back into my purse. "You can't do this. Not again. Never again."

More reason to leave. Now. Before it was too late.

But what about Ty? What if he came back and didn't find me?

He left you. He's never coming back. He's never coming back to you.

That inner voice nagged at me, but my mind refused to believe he'd just leave without even saying goodbye. Part of me was still wishing for his return, even if we should have never been together, even if we would never be again.

No. He had to come back eventually, even if it wasn't for me, and I'd wait. Running away now would only incite more suspicions, if there were any in Furore's head, anyway. I had to stay put and pretend nothing had happened, at least, until I knew for sure the vague threats behind his words were empty.

Lying back in bed, I sighed against the pillow. Would my life ever get easier?

I begged for sleep to swallow me. Suddenly, the nightmares felt like the lesser evil tonight. But when I closed my eyes, all I could see was Ty's face. I couldn't bring myself to blink it away. I didn't have any pictures of him or us together to go to when missing him was too much to bear; it was too risky. My memories were the only proof of his existence and the time we'd had together. Those I vowed never to forget. I'd forever cherish them even if they were wrong or never meant to be.

"Hush, baby. I'm here. It's safe," he'd have said.

"But you're not here anymore."

Just close your eyes and dream of me.

My wet lashes drooped and let the dark surround me. I filled my nostrils with his smell I conjured from memory and wrapped my arms around myself, pretending it was him enfolding me. "Can you sing it?"

Anything for you, Miss Meneceo.

I chuckled. He loved to call me Miss Meneceo, especially in bed. God, it was hot.

But if you laugh at my accent again…

"You know I will."

Well, laugh all you want, Miss Meneceo. You know what you're up for if you do.

"No, I don't." I lied. I knew exactly what he'd have done. "Just sing."

Over in Killarney
Many years ago
Me mother sang a song to me
In tones so sweet and low
Just a simple little ditty
In her good old Irish way
And I'd give the world to hear her sing
That song of hers today

Tears rolled down my cheeks, slowly soaking my pillow sheet. I rocked myself like he'd have done, his voice echoing in my head as he pulled the best Irish accent he could muster just for me.

Too-ra-loo-ra-loo-ral, Too-ra-loo-ra-li
Too-ra-loo-ra-loo-ral, hush now, don't you cry
Too-ra-loo-ra-loo-ral, Too-ra-loo-ra-li

I'm here and will never say goodbye, singing you an Irish lullaby

My heart ached. "That's not how the last line goes."

I know. Gotta make it my own.

"But you left me, Ty."

Too-ra-loo-ra-loo-ral, hush now, don't you cry

Too-ra-loo-ra-loo-ral, Too-ra-loo-ra-li…

Wait…are you laughing?

"You have the worst Irish accent ever."

His grunt of what would have been disapproval murmured in my ears, sending a sweet shudder down my core. *Don't say I didn't warn you. Bad girls like you don't get lullabied to sleep. They get fucked to sleep. On your stomach. Now.*

I flipped over, my fingers slipping inside my panties. I was so wet and ready for him. God, I missed him. Missed the heat of his lean, firm body cascading over my skin, missed watching the angry cords of his muscles in his neck and shoulders tensing as his hands dug into my flesh, missed the thickness of him filling me all night as he relentlessly pounded me until we were both satisfied and worn out.

Ty didn't just fuck me to sleep. He fucked the demons out until there was nothing left but the two of us and the peace that came after.

My fingers were nothing compared to the magic he wielded with his cock, but I moved fast, rubbing my clit, my teeth spearing my lips as heat gathered in my belly and pushed lower.

I fucking love your cunt. Love the way you take me, Jo. Fuck, you're such a slut taking all of me like that, Miss Meneceo.

Moans seeped out of my throat and met the wet sounds my pussy made around my fingers. *I want you to look at me.* I rolled on my back to see his face as if he were here. *Look at how you're taking my cock, Jo.*

I gasped loudly, my back arching, my pelvis in the air reaching, begging for him. *I fucking love you, Jo. Fucking love you…*

Jo.

My eyes snapped open as, suddenly, it wasn't Ty's voice or face in my head. It wasn't his lips that said my name. It was Furore's.

C'mon, don't be shy now. I know you want me like I want you.

"What the fuck?" I gasped at the empty darkness, my mind playing a slideshow of one picture on repeat. Laius Lazzarini's lips puckering up and whispering my name, slowly, teasingly, sensually.

Be a good girl and finish yourself off for me...Jo.

Abruptly, dark green eyes framed in gray taunting me, my body clenched and an orgasm crashed over me hard.

Ci vediamo, Jo.

CHAPTER 4

FURORE

Time on the yard didn't take my mind off that darn class. The burn in my muscles didn't rid myself of the rage the brunette bitch had sparked within me when she dared insinuate I was no match for her brains, lying to my face, looking down on me without even knowing me. I did get back at her, acting like I didn't give a rat's ass, calling her on her shit, but I was still raging. No one spoke to me like that. I ate bitches like her for breakfast. And lunch. And dinner.

"Going hard on the weights today, ain't we, Furore? What's pissin' ya?" Maverick, a piece of shit runner for Lanza's Mob, hunkered down next me, a slimy smile on his fucking face.

What was really pissing me more than her fucking attitude was something I wouldn't admit to myself, let alone to some motherfucking mafia bitch. The unbelievable wild lust that five hundred sit-ups and a hundred pounds of heavy lifting couldn't shake. The hunger that slammed into me once she thought she could challenge me, and the fucking desire that shot through me during that flicker of a touch… Fuck.

I was supposed to fidget *her* up with that touch, not the other way around. That buzz that traveled between us had been so unexpected it caught me off guard. Damn, I missed my bike and the club whores that lined up to suck this stupid shit out of me. Since that spiteful bitch I'd made my ol' lady framed me, sent my ass to the slammer the first time, took my baby boy and left the whole state to whore herself and land a richer motherfucker, I trusted no damn creature with a cunt. And every time I came close to feeling anything, and I meant anything, that could be mistakenly taken for any kind of affection toward a woman, I rode long and fucked hard until none of it was left.

Could you blame me? Fifteen years later, and my ass was shoved behind bars again because of that Delilah bitch. If it wasn't for my boy, I would have killed the switch on that bitch the second she betrayed me. But I couldn't do that to my son. He was only three, and the club was a mess. Who would have taken care of him? Delilah was shitty as fuck and had poisoned him with lies that made him hate me till today, but, at least, she took care of him.

And if it wasn't for my boy, I wouldn't have dragged my ass to the bitch's house here, had a *word* with the fucking husband she'd gotten herself. A spineless motherfucker who beat the shit out of her for sport. I didn't give a fuck about her, but the second I heard the son of a bitch tried to land a hand on my boy, I got burning acid for blood.

I gave the chicken shit a lesson he wouldn't forget and a mark that would stay for life, if he managed to get out of the hospital alive. I'd have gotten away with it if that bitch didn't call the fucking pigs on me. Again.

But here I was, wasting two more years of my life in a fucking can, getting a boner, to a hot, pompous ass teacher of all the people in the world, that would have nothing by my fist to take care of, sharing a yard with slimy worms like Maverick Alfonso, because of that cunt.

And the worst part was my son wouldn't even talk to me. I'd been sending him letters for four months now, since I got in San Quentin, but I hadn't received a single reply.

Other than 'fuck off. I never want to see you or any of your brothers ever again' he hadn't said a word to me in fifteen years. He even blamed me for what I did to Delilah's husband, saying he'd never asked for my help, and that piece of shit was the only dad he'd ever known.

A growl blasted out of my throat as I pushed the weights up and down faster. Maverick—who in their fucking right mind chose a pussy ass name like Maverick to be their street name? Or was it really the name his parents gave him? Shit. No wonder he was such a loser—straightened up, casting a shadow over my head. "Hey, easy. You're gonna hurt yerself. That bitch gave you an F or what?" He snickered. "Is that what got you all wrathy?"

Bile rose to my throat just listening to the fucker. "No. I just miss fucking your mama's hairy cunt."

He snorted a laugh that sounded like a fucking hyena choking. "Nah. Bet it's another cunt that got your balls in a knot."

Don't talk about her cunt. I didn't know where that came from, but it pissed the shit out of me. I dropped the fucking weights with a bang on the ground and let my sweat drip on that ugly ass for a face of his. "I wish, but it's your mama's cunt that I miss so much I'll pound the first thing that looks like it. Bet your fucking stinky ass will do."

He flinched, holding his hands up. "Hey, don't shoot the messenger. I'm just checkin' if you got something for my boss."

"When your boss wanted something from me, he came to me direct. He didn't send a motherfucking worm to sniff around."

"But you wouldn't wanna cost him the trip down here only to send him home empty-handed."

"Tell your boss I'm working on it. This shit takes time."

"With a pretty motherfucker like you, it shouldn't take that long. Just sayin', everybody is talking about how you got a little alone time with the fat back teach. But her sunglasses never left her face, and you were passing notes and shit. Capo won't like it if he finds out that alone time is for nothing…or worse."

I grabbed him by the collar of his shirt and brought him toward me and squeezed my other hand around his shoulder as if we were having a talk and I wasn't about to smash the shit out of his face. "The fuck that means?" I practically spat in his ear.

He was shaking. "Did you tip the bitch?"

"Fuck you, dipshit." I didn't know what infuriated me more, the fact that he thought I was a rat, stupid enough to warn the oblivious teacher about the danger she was in, out in the open where anyone could see, or that he called her a bitch…and fat back…and mentioned her cunt on his disgusting tongue.

That made me even angrier. I got why I wanted to do wicked things to her all over her desk until she knew how I expected to be treated. But why the fuck would I care if he or any other fucker called her shit or jacked off to her hot ass? It made me want to beat the shit out of something—might as well be that worm—until blood covered us both.

"Just lookin' out for you, bro. Don't want you wasting your free out of jail ticket back to H-town." His disgusting mouth drooled as he burst out in laughter. "See what I did here? Switched card for ticket 'cause that what gets you home and what not. A little creative, don't you think? Enough to maybe take that fine ass class myself. Then it won't be so hard to just snatch those sunglasses the bitch is hiding behind and see what color eye she's got. It'll be all the proof we need. Ya know, I put ten squares on *Irish* eyes. Should do the same. Earn a little something on the side 'cause maybe you won't be getting out of here that soon after all."

My hand fisted around his shoulder, squeezing until something cracked and he yelped like a little pussy. "First, I'm not your fucking bro. Second, don't ever fucking think you can threaten me. Third, like I said, your boss came to *me* for what he wanted, not to a dumbfuck, piece of shit runner like you, even when he owned your ass. So you tell him, if he still wants me digging that juice on the girl, he'll make as many trips down here as needed to get what he's looking for 'cause from now on, your little messenger ass is fucking barred. You hear me, bitch? You see me anywhere, you fucking run." I eased my grip, the fucker shaking like a wet dog, nodding his head. "Starting now."

He ran to his Mickey Mouse borgata like a scared shitless little girl. I stood, waiting to see if any of his amici was going to come over and start some shit, itching for some action, but all they did was some eyeballing before

they took their worm under their wings and
left.

CHAPTER 5

FURORE

Three Weeks Ago

When they said I had a visitor, I wished
it'd have been my boy finally agreeing
to see me or just coming to give me
shit about what I'd done, but it was likely one
of the brothers updating me on business or a
sweet butt coming to give me some company
and show me a little bit of what I'd been
missing.

What was waiting at the table, though, was a suit as expensive as my bike on a shiny scarface with enough grease in his hair to butter up an entire engine.

He smiled like we were best friends, not two strangers that were meeting for the first time. "If it isn't the infamous Laius Lazzarini himself. Piacere."

I narrowed my gaze at him, sizing him up. "The name is Furore."

"Certo. Furore it is. I'm Armando L—"

"I know who you are." I pushed my elbows on the table and tilted my chin up. "The new coyote."

He gave a low laugh. "Word travels fast. Do you know my cousin?"

"Can't say that I do." All I knew was Domenico Lanza was the Lanza famiglia enforcer and a motherfucking bastard that flayed his enemies and fed them to the coyotes. That was how he got the name Il Coyote. Last winter, he had an *accident* and had to *retire* early. At least, that was the story the Mafia lords of San Francisco were feeding everyone. But the rumors were—more than rumors if you asked me—shit hit the fan between the Lanzas and their best buddies and recently in-laws, the Bellomos—the Mafia lords that ran Chicago. Domenico Lanza paid the price. Some said the son of a bitch had it coming. Others were sobbing tears over the Italian Dom. Me? Didn't give a shit. Never would I over a Mafioso. I cared about no one but my own family. The Night Skulls and my own blood. "To what do I owe the pleasure of your precious visit?"

A cocky smirk curved his mouth. "As you know, the Night Skulls and the Lanzas have always been good friends."

"Maybe with the San Francisco chapter, which, *as you know*, is a fucking memory. One we don't like to remember."

He chuckled. "Not just with that chapter. The ones all over Europe are still great allies to the Lanzas. We'd like to be friends with the chapters in Texas, too. You're the man that can make that happen."

I didn't like where this was going. Running with the Mob was shitty business, and I'd managed to stay out of it until now. Besides, the Lanzas ran the west coast. Since when did they or any mobster have interest in the South where gambling was a shit show? *Why are we really having this conversation, Lanza?* "I only run Houston."

"C'mon, Furore. We all know you're their leader. You even have significant weight with the rivals. If there's one man that can get the South under one call, it's you."

This wasn't about getting friendly with the Night Skulls. This was about easing a way in to a new turf. A connection that could build a bridge that would lead not to the MCs or the casinos but straight to the cartel. Looked like the rumors weren't horseshit after all, and no matter how the two families were trying to sugarcoat it, the Lanzas and the Bellomos honeymoon was over. The Lanzas had lost their cut in the Midwest, and they wanted to get their hands on a new territory. Yeah, I didn't like where this was going. No one in the South would.

But you didn't say that with a straight face to a fucking Mafioso, especially when you had twenty-one months more to serve in a fucking can. "When I'm out of here, I'll be happy to discuss said friendship with you and pass it to the other presidents in our quarterly church. We'll vote on it."

The arrogant smile he had on vanished as he slowly leaned forward. "How's your son doing, Furore?"

Was this little shit trying to threaten me? Leveraging my own boy against me? It was one thing to keep my shit for the sake of keeping business going without unnecessary wars, but when it came to my own family, I didn't give a fuck. A mafia enforcer with an army behind him or not, nobody threatened my family.

"*Piano*." He must have read my face and got the hint because he was flashing his *friendly* smile again, asking me to take it easy. "I mean, I'm sure you'd like to get out of here as soon as possible and try for a family reunion with him. Two years seem a little too long. You must miss him."

I squinted at him. "Twenty-one months."

"When you put it that way it sounds even longer. I don't know, but if I were you, I'd do anything that could get me out of here in, say, three months, or…maybe even now."

Taking a deep breath, I blinked. So it wasn't a threat but an offer? "No judge will reduce the sentence to six months because of my priors and how that filthy fuck is connected. I was lucky to get just two years. It could have been four. That bitch called the cops on me herself and said I was gonna kill both her and her wife beater of a husband. I didn't even point that gun at either of them, but her testimony stood."

"It's just words, Furore. She can change them."

"She's my boy's mother. I won't let any—"

"I figured you'd say that, and I respect you for it. Still, what if I can tell you our lawyers can make what you've done look like self-defense and get you out of here in no time?"

My brows hooked. "Without getting anywhere near Delilah?"

He nodded once.

"How?"

"McNamara is on our dime. Well, his aunt is."

"His aunt? The mayor?"

"She's a great lady. I never liked the nephew, though. I think that's something we both can agree on. I'm glad you taught that motherfucker a lesson. As a matter of fact, I think you went easy on him."

"That asshole won't walk straight again. I broke half of his bones."

"Exactly. He got lucky."

I scratched the back of my head, getting the info soaked in. "That's why I got two years instead of four, ain't that right?"

"Smart fella. And if you do us that one little favor, we'll make McNamara himself say he threw the first punch and his bitch was lying."

That was how much power the Lanzas had on their turf. They would make the mayor's nephew, who was still lying in a fucking hospital till today, drop the case like the little chicken shit he was, and even the mayor couldn't help him because she was in the Mafia's pocket.

I wiped my mouth and beard, deep in thought. Getting out of the slammer now, trying to win my boy back before that bitch poisoned him further against me, was more than tempting. There was nothing I wanted more than to have my son by my side. My odds at having that were slimmer by the day. He was eighteen now. One more year in high school, and with his brains, he'd go off to college with no hustle. He'd be madder and more embarrassed of me, and the next thing I knew, his kids wouldn't even know who their real grandpa was. I didn't want that to happen. He was my only son. I'd always wanted to be in his life, taking care of him, protecting him, loving him. I wanted to teach him how to ride, give him his first bike, be there for his graduation and wedding, and get his little suckers Christmas presents.

That bitch took his past from me. I shouldn't let her ruin the future, too. "That little favor is my vote when I pass your proposal to the other presidents?"

He shook his head, his smile growing wider. "No, Furore. That would be for the two-year sentence. For the acquittal, there's something else."

My fist clenched under the table. I hated those mafia fucks. They thought they owned everything and could force anyone to play their game the way they wanted, only the way they wanted. Fuck that shit. He thought he owned me for a favor I didn't ask for? He didn't know who he was fucking with, but for my boy, I'd pretend I took the bait. "Let's hear it."

A triumphant look glistened on his face. Seriously, that guy was shinier than a sleek, brand new bike on a hot, sunny day. Even the scar that ran on the side of his nose and down to his upper lip seemed transparent. That was how fucking clean he was. What did those motherfuckers eat? "There's a woman who teaches here. We have reasons to believe she's not who she says she is. We want you to verify that for us," he said, his voice lower by an octave I could barely hear him over the noises of the other inmates.

The fuck? "Huh?"

"You heard me the first time. Her name is—"

"Meneceo. I know all about the hot teach every fucker is wanking off to these days. They talk about nothing but her hot ass and the shades she wears all the time like she's a fucking Fed. There's even a bet going around—"

"About what color her eyes are," he interrupted me like I interrupted him, his gaze letting me know he didn't appreciate it when I did. "We know. But we'd like to have that piece of information earlier than anyone else and keep it exclusive for as long as possible."

"Why?"

"We're curious if the little Italian high school teacher has Irish eyes. It's important to be the first to know if it's true."

Blinking, I tried to put two and two together, but I couldn't place it. Let's say she was Irish hiding under an Italian name for whatever fucking reason, why did they care? Why was it urgent information? And why would they come to me to figure it out for them? Why wouldn't they just send any of their men to find out the stupid color of her eyes out there, bribe one of her friends or even a kid at the school where she taught? "I don't get it."

"The less you know the better. All we need you to do is charm her, get her to trust you enough to talk a little about her past. Any detail no matter how small will help. And most importantly, make her show you her eyes." He smirked. "I have no doubt you can make her show you more than that."

I rolled my eyes with a chuckle. "I still don't get it. You can't be serious about the eyes. So many people have light blue eyes, but they're not really Irish. It proves nothing."

He reached inside the pocket of his suit jacket and brought out a photo. He leaned forward and stretched his arms as he slid the photo across the table for me to see, making sure it was only me that could see it. "When you see them, you'll know."

I took a hint, so I didn't touch the photo and only dropped my eyes a little so no one around would notice. The second my gaze met the innocent, most eccentric, light greenish blue eyes I'd ever seen, ones that were so unique it was almost impossible for even God to remake, I froze, my lips parting with a silent gasp. I, a grown ass motherfucker, fucking gasped, and no air came in or out because that little blonde girl's face in the photo literally took my breath away.

Then something vicious and dangerous clicked in me. The girl in the photo couldn't have been more than ten years old. Maybe even younger. So beautiful and innocent and clueless…and sad, so sad. I didn't know if it

nature of this conversation but you and me. Your discretion, which I know you'll honor, is very much appreciated."

I snorted. "Trust easy, huh?"

"What are friends if they can't trust each other, goombah?" He rose, buttoning his suit jacket. "Besides, I'm sure you know that if we can make McNamara move his tongue to say the right words, we can also make him shut his mouth forever. How much time do you think people serve for manslaughter in here? With your priors and him being the mayor's nephew… Good God, they can push for life. Che guaio. Shit would be really hard on you, and your poor son would lose both his fathers. I wouldn't want that for you or him."

CHAPTER 6

JO

I didn't know what possessed me to masturbate to Laius Lazzarini. A convict. An outlaw that headed one of the most vicious, one-percenter motorcycle clubs in the country, perhaps even in the world.

Anybody who lived in California long enough, especially in San Francisco, knew what the Night Skulls were and what they did in America and Europe. There were horror stories about the criminal activities and abductions the San Francisco chapter was involved in before its destruction a few years ago, in the fire that allegedly killed all the members that were at their compound in Rosewood.

I wouldn't even begin to delude myself about the nature of the Houston chapter and their president. He was in prison for beating a man almost to death, threatening a woman at gunpoint and almost killing them if she didn't call the cops in time. No logic could justify my ghastly attraction to such a brutal criminal.

Except attraction needed no logic and knew no rules or boundaries.

My heart squeezed as my gaze roamed around the foreign periodical section—the most secluded section—at the back of the school library. Where my first kiss was stolen from me. Where I first lost all common sense and caution and broke all the rules.

It'd been a cold day, and the nightmares had been having a field day with me. After several coffees, I'd managed to teach my classes until fourth period. Then exhaustion overwhelmed me. The teacher's lounge was too loud and crowded, so I'd used my lunch time to come to the library and rest. Wrong? Maybe, but my other options had been either the toilet or my car. Both would have been freezing and not a nice look for me if I'd been caught. The library had been the safest option. No one went to that aisle unless they were about to have sex. I'd convinced myself I was doing the school a favor by being there to scare away the students—and teachers—who had had any intension to exploit the space for *nonacademic activities*. How virtuous of me, right?

Using my jacket as a pillow, I'd dozed off at the secluded aisle. It'd been the best sleep I'd had in months. Until a warm breath had whispered in my ear, waking me up.

"You're so beautiful. So fucking beautiful," a voice had been whispering. No one had ever called me beautiful in a whisper before. It'd felt like a dream. A good one for a change. I didn't want to wake up.

Something had feathered down my cheekbone and along my jawline, sending a shiver down my spine and a clench between my thighs. This couldn't have been right. I never had good dreams, let alone wet ones…that had felt so real. My eyes had snapped open, and I'd seen it.

His heart melting smile that had had the girls in Raoul Sala High swooning met my startled gaze. I blinked at his tattooed hand that was withdrawing from my face, leaving me more confused. Had he really touched me?

"I didn't mean to startle you, Miss Meneceo." The dark green abysses had held me immobile, being that close—too close for my sanity—for the first time. That voice that didn't belong to a boy but a man, a very masculine man, was even more *distracting* when it whispered. "I was just checking if you were all right. You looked so peaceful when you were sleeping."

"Tirone." I'd blinked hard, frowning, his smell mixed with that of his leather jacket, filling the very little air he'd allowed between us. He'd been squatting in front of me on the floor, his arms stretched by my side as he'd held the shelf behind me, caging me in that little space. "You're not supposed to be here. What are you... What—"

"Hushh. We're in the library," he'd said playfully. "You don't want someone to come here and think..."

"Think what?" I'd lowered my voice in shock.

"That we snuck here to do what people actually come to do in this aisle."

I'd gaped at him. "Oh my God. Are you out of your mind? This is inappropriate even as a joke, so is your presence here...like that. You have to go. Now," I'd said as firmly as possible.

His eyes had traveled from my face down to my neck, and then to my chest. "You should put on your jacket. I don't want anyone to see you like that."

Frowning, I'd looked down at my blouse. Instantly, my eyes had widened. A button must have come undone in my sleep because I'd seen my bra and half of my breasts from that view and he must have, too.

My mouth too dry to swallow, I'd grabbed my jacket and stood. He'd moved with me, his arms still forming that cage around me, his height towering over me. I'd pressed the jacket to my chest to cover up. "Tirone, move out of the way."

"Not until I do this."

Before I could have opened my mouth to ask, heat had scorched my lips. It'd taken me a moment to register Tirone Wisely's lips, my student's lips, were on mine, sending flutters in my heart, sucking all my power, swallowing me in flames.

Without knowing, giving me my first kiss. Or rather stealing it.

I'd been too dazed by the flooding sensations and searing inferno erupting through my body to stop him right away, and for one unholy moment, my brain had shut down and my ovaries took over, urging me to let him finish what he started without interruptions.

Just for one moment. Then my palm had found his cheek in a slap.

Stunned, we both had stared at each other. I was desperate for my sunglasses to hide behind them, but in foggy San Francisco, I couldn't wear them all the time, especially in winter. I'd worn my contacts that day. Brown. But I'd felt he'd seen right through them, right through me. His face was so red, with shock, shame or anger, I hadn't known, but I'd had no doubt mine was even redder with all of those. "What the hell have you done? Are you crazy?"

"Yes," he'd hissed. "*You* have been driving me crazy for months. Months, Jo."

"What?"

"*If I were to kiss you then go to hell, I would. So then I can brag with the devils I saw heaven without ever entering it.* All those essays and poems you've made us write, how could you not know mine were all about you? How could you be so oblivious?"

I'd shaken my head vigorously, equally disturbed and in awe. "I'm your teacher, and you're a student. How could you—"

"I don't give a shit."

"I do," I'd said through my teeth. "And so does the law. This is wrong and illegal."

"Only if we get caught, but I won't let that happen."

"Tirone, move or I'll report you."

He'd smirked, letting his knuckles brush down my cheek. "No, you won't. You care about me like I care about you." He'd licked his bottom lip and let out a little groan that unexpectedly and sinfully vibrated through my core. "You loved that kiss as much as I did."

I'd slapped his hand off me. "Yes, I will. What you've done is a crime. You touched me without consent. You forced your mouth—"

"If you play that way, it's gonna be your word against mine."

My jaw had dropped. "Excuse me?"

"I'd say you told me to meet you here."

"You little piece of shit. You think you can come here, take whatever you want without asking, and then threaten me, and I'll just do nothing?"

"Fuck. You're so hot when you're pissed."

"You're insane."

"Yes, I'm insane. Because of you. I've never been like this, but since you set foot in our school… I've been fighting for an entire semester, Jo, but I couldn't get you out of my mind. So I decided, this semester, I'd tell you.

I've been trying to make you understand, but you won't. This was the only way."

I should have been appalled and disturbed by his inappropriate declarations. I should have pushed him away and gone through with my threat to report him. I should have never ever thought that was the sweetest and hottest thing a boy had ever told me. "You need help, Tirone." So did I.

"All I need is you, Jo. *That hugest whole creation may be less incalculable than one kiss*...and in that kiss, I knew you needed me, too. "

My eyes had burned with the tears that suddenly had sprung in them and with the irritation from the contacts had been about to spill. How could I have been so weak to lose myself even for one moment? How could I have been mesmerized that he was citing E. E. Cummings after that disgrace? How could have one moment been enough for him to know? "That's not true." I had to lie.

"Don't try to lie to yourself or me because I felt you. I know when a woman wants me, Jo. There's nothing wrong with a woman needing a man, especially when that man is crazy for her."

No one had ever told me something like that before. I was twenty-two and had never been in a relationship, serious or otherwise.

Not even a fleeting crush. A couple of minutes ago, I hadn't even known what a kiss felt like. Then, Tirone Wisely, one of the sexiest boys in school had told me he was crazy for me.

My mind had been about to take a break again, but I hadn't let it. I couldn't have. Not again. "You're not a man. You're a boy." I'd shaken at the words, as if the weight of their meaning suddenly had dawned on me. "A minor."

Anger had flashed on his face "I'm not a boy. I'm almost eighteen, Jo."

He didn't look or taste like a boy. He was gorgeous and exuded enough masculinity to fill ten men. But it didn't change the fact of what he truly was. "My name is Miss Meneceo. Even if you're eighteen, I'm still your teacher. This can't ever happen again." I'd been scolding myself, not him. "Now, get out of the way because I swear to God if you don't, I'll scream right here right now and won't care what happens next to either of us."

Hurt and distraught and raging, the look in his beautiful eyes had held me in place long enough to shake me. I'd wondered if he'd have let me go or would have touched me again, against all common sense, against my will. I'd wondered if I'd have fought and screamed like I'd said I'd have. I was glad he had dropped his stare and arms because my resolve wouldn't have lasted long enough.

I'd moved two steps before he hauled me back against the shelf, and I'd have sworn he'd have kissed me again. Part of me, wicked and shameless, wanted him to. My heart had gone frantic when his fingers had found the fabric of my blouse, the back of his hand teasing the skin between my breasts, leaving a line of fire in their wake. I'd opened my mouth to speak, to protest, but nothing had come out but an embarrassing gasp.

"I told you I didn't want anyone to see you like that. Your body is for my eyes only, *Jo*." He'd fixed my button. "You want us to wait? Fine, I'll wait, but until then you're mine. If I see anyone, and I mean anyone, coming near you, I'll punch the shit out of them and fuck you right in front of everybody if I have to so that they'll lay off my girl. I won't give a fuck if you scream or report me or call the fucking cops. I'll ruin us both without a single regret because it'll still make you mine. Do you hear me, Jo? You're mine."

I closed my eyes like I'd had in that moment, savoring every ridiculous jealous possessive word that had been ruining me for months, chest heaving with all the forbidden feelings that still engulfed my body and heart...

"Jo? Earth to Jo?"

With a flinch, I opened my eyes and tilted my head toward the direction of the voice that snapped me out of the haunting memory. Jarica Williams. A Biology teacher. She must have come to meet her students at the library like I had. We both taught the dreaded summer courses.

Immediately, she started complaining about Mr. Perez's selecting her for teaching the course. To every other teacher, being forced by the principal to be here in the summer was a miserable chore. For me, it was a different story. I volunteered, just like I did in San Quentin.

"Bless your heart, Jo," she wheezed a little, wiping the sweat off her forehead. "Such a nice girl. A do-gooder. I don't know why you haven't scored a man yet. You're kind, young, beautiful and look at all what you're giving back to society."

I laughed under my breath. If only she knew. "Thank you, Mrs. Williams." I didn't do either volunteer job out of the goodness of my heart, though. In San Quentin, I was doing it to atone. The summer course I was doing as a last hope.

Ty disappeared one week before his exams. He never took them. I was hoping he'd come for the summer courses. My heart had leapt when I saw his name on the list, and I was ripped to shreds when he still didn't show.

"Do you know what happened to that boy?" she asked.

My heart skipped a beat. "Which boy?" I knew exactly whom, but I played dumb.

"Tyron Wisely."

"You mean Tirone," I corrected because he hated it when people couldn't pronounce his name correctly. It was one of the things we had in common, and we used to laugh about it together all the time. He'd resorted to being called Ty—even though technically Tee was how his name was to be shortened—because no matter what they kept called him Tyron.

"Yes, Tirone Wisely. What a waste. He was brilliant. I couldn't believe he just dropped out."

"Me neither." Despite the risk, I'd driven to his place and even rung the bell. If either of his parents had opened the door, I could have just said I was there to see why he hadn't showed up at school, and that I'd been concerned about his future as a good, caring teacher.

But no one was there. The house was empty. There were rumors that he skipped town with his family after someone had broken into their house. If that was true, why didn't he call me or return my calls, at least, to let me know he was okay? I'd been worried sick. And how was such incident a reason to drop out of school right before his exams? He could have easily asked to be tested online from the safety of his new home. Something else happened, and I couldn't help thinking I had a hand in it.

Guilt raptured through me all day, as it had all year, and more guilt followed me into the next week when my loneliness at night had made me resort to yet another forbidden deed. That first night I came hard to Furore wasn't the last. Every time I touched myself, thinking about Ty, the only man that had ever touched me, the only man that captivated my heart and never let go, I ended up seeing Furore's eyes, hearing him whispering my name, commanding me to come for him, and my body obeyed. As if I could no longer get wet except for tattooed, dark green-eyed students of mine. Ones that made me fear them as much as I'd been attracted to them.

At San Quentin, I waited behind my desk in the classroom for the inmates to arrive, sweating on an uncharacteristically cool summer afternoon for no good reason except my fear of being exposed. For what I'd been doing every night for the past week—as if Furore would take one look at me and know. And for whom I really was.

Our uncomfortable exchange last week hadn't gone unforgotten. He was a criminal with a piece of information, though simple, he shouldn't have had access to. Who knew how he'd intended to use it against me? Blackmail? Coercion? And to whose favor?

Then there was the matter of his son. I was curious to know the story behind him. Perhaps when I knew, I'd unravel a secret of Furore's myself, and we'd both have equal leverage against each other.

That was why today, even though he'd pushed past the other inmates, sat in his desk without saying a word, not even a simple greeting, and buried his nose in his notebook, ignoring my presence as if I was insignificant, the next assignment would force him out of his disrespectful silence.

CHAPTER 7

JO

"In no less than fifty words, I'd like you to revisit your first assignment. Do you remember that one?" I stood at the back of the class for the announcement, where the guard was, preparing for the worst.

"The swearing thing?" Laniakea guessed.

"No," I chuckled.

"Damn. The why you're here assignment?"

"We all know why you're here. You stole a goddamn TV," Ren Sanchez said. "Ain't you learn fucking nothing from Shawshank, man?"

Laughter hummed in the classroom. While I enjoyed the banter, I didn't appreciate bad grammar or ignoring my rules. *"Haven't you learned anything from this class, Ren? And remember what I said about swearing?"*

"Sorry, Miss M. I shall write it down in the most creative way to the best of my abilities." He snickered.

"Apology accepted." I ignored the mockery *to the best of my abilities.* It came with an eye roll, though. "Now back to the assignment. Yes, it is the one where I told you to write your ultimate goal you hoped to achieve by enrolling in this class." Which Furore had dodged with his bravado and intimidating tactics. "Now, write down how after four weeks of education you're getting closer to your goal. The skills you've truly learned, the difference you can feel, the measures you'll take to be better and achieve your goal, and most importantly," my gaze drifted to the back of Furore's head involuntarily, "what truly motivates you to keep going."

Heads tilted toward me, but my focus was with the one that didn't turn.

Say something. Challenge me. Smirk at me. Warn me with a stare. Throw a tantrum. Anything.

Without so much of a pause, Furore was the first to open his notebook and start writing.

"All right. You have fifteen minutes. Any questions, I'm right here." My lips twisted with inexplicable irritation. The whole point of the assignment was to get him to write. To spill his secrets about his son and how my class was going to help with whatever his real goal was. To get leverage. Why was I angry? Why did it bother me that he was ignoring me? Why would I be irritated if a student stopped provoking me and started working on his tasks? Because that was what Laius Lazzarini was. A student. No matter how hard it was for me to ignore the intoxicating dominant presence of the man who had been driving me crazy for days, I must not see him in any other way.

"Miss Meneceo, a word please," the guard said.

I rolled my eyes over to him. He'd never spoken to me before other than to emphasize security instructions. Now, he had something to say me? Could he not see I'd sharpened my emotional and intellectual claws, and it was all for nothing? I was in the middle of a psychological war game I had to win. What

could be so important? "Yes…" I realized I
didn't even know his name.

"I…I just want to say that…" His mouth
twitched with a smile, which would have been
beautiful if it wasn't nervous. "Um…am I
allowed to say you look lovely today?"

My lashes fluttered for a second, and then
warmth touched my cheeks as his eyes—
which I'd noticed for the first time were blue,
by the way—wandered to my hair. I didn't do
the usual ponytail or bun and put my hair
down today. "Oh." I touched the back of my
hair, averting my gaze. "Thank you…" I
didn't know what else to say. Was he flirting
with me? I understood nothing in this
department. Should I return the compliment?
He was wearing his usual uniform, and he had
a buzz cut covered by a cap. I didn't even
know his name, so I glanced up at the tag.
"…Guard Murphy."

"My name is David."

Oh my God. He was flirting. Fuck.
"Pleasure. My name is Jo." Fuck.

He laughed quietly. "I know."

"Of course you do." I looked away, hoping
a student would ask a question and give me an
excuse to end this awkward conversation.

"Hey, I was…wondering if maybe
you…wanna grab a cup of coffee sometime."

No.

The answer popped in my head on autopilot, out of fear I should no longer have, and was about to jump out of my tongue if I hadn't curbed it on time.

There was no reason for me to be rude. He was just a nice person asking me out. There was no reason for me to be afraid. The jealous, possessive, borderline psycho boyfriend—the only boyfriend—I had dumped my ass months ago without even bothering to break up with me. Even if I hadn't been over him yet, even if I'd been spending my mornings thinking about him and my nights crying and longing for him, I shouldn't have been rude to a guy who seemed to be interested in me or afraid of what Ty might have done if he'd known.

I was a single woman now. It was completely fine to receive such requests. It'd be absolutely fine if I chose to accept them, too. Ty, obviously, didn't care anymore. He wouldn't have left if he had.

"Um…I…" I forced a smile out, even though I wanted to cry, my cheeks burning now. How pathetic was I? A man was telling me I looked nice and was asking me out, and I was about to burst into tears because I couldn't get over the boy that broke my heart.

The one I should have never been with or wanted back. The one I still waited for his return like a sad, pitiful, stupid woman with no dignity or shame.

"Miss Meneceo, I have a question."

My whole body shifted focus toward what was painstakingly the sexiest voice I'd ever heard and the man who owned it. *Oh, so his tongue wasn't cut off or no one hit him on the head that he forgot how to form words or anything that would stop him from returning a simple good morning to his teacher?* "Yes, Laius."

He'd finally looked at me, his eyes a heating menace. "Could you be kind enough to come check the spelling of this word for me?"

And look at those words. How so polite of Furore. Is he a gentleman now? "It's not a spelling bee competition." I didn't know why I said that. Why I had to provoke him, when I should pacify him. In my defense, it was the only act I was used to. Do anything to keep people away. Be cold and distant. Intimidate. Irritate. The more I was afraid the worse it got. It was no secret I was afraid of Laius Lazzarini, for reasons more than one.

Inmates started the usual sneering whenever I came back at one of them. I gave them the *stare*. "Just write the paragraph. Same goes for all of you. I won't deduct any marks for spelling mistakes."

Furore narrowed his eyes at me, hard. "But for this word, the wrong spelling could lead to a different meaning. I want to make sure you understand me correctly with no confusion, *Miss Meneceo*."

I swallowed at the tone of his voice, at the command in it, at the threat it held, at the seduction it carried whenever he drawled my name like that.

Glancing at Murphy, I gave him a tight nod to excuse me for the interruption. Then I took a deep breath and went over to Furore's desk. "What word?"

He stared at my breasts when I bent to see his notebook, so blatantly sweat hit my armpits and waves of heat flooded my neck. I glared at him, even though he couldn't see my eyes. I was sure my face conveyed the message. His jaw twisted and shook his head once as if he was the one who should be upset, as if he had the right to undress me with his eyes without a single complaint on my side. He pointed his pencil to a line he'd written. "Here."

I took another deep breath, convincing myself to ignore his misconducts for now to go on with my plan and get what I needed. I rolled my eyes toward the notebook.

Stop talking to the guard. I don't like it.

My brow shot high in my forehead, and fury—along with surprise— surged in me. "Excuse me?"

He gave me a menacing stare. A warning so I'd keep quiet and play his game without exposing him. I shouldn't heed his warning. I should call for Murphy, who was eyeing us like a hawk, ready to pounce.

But I wouldn't. Not yet.

"That's a very inappropriate *word* to use," I said. "The whole *argument* is." Who was he to make such demand? Who was he whether to like when I spoke to the guard or not? And above all, why did he not like it? "Why are you inclined to make it?"

His jaws clenched, and his eyes returned to roam my body with something I recognized. Something that had once burned in similar eyes and scorched me with its intensity. Something that had drowned me in searing sin beyond absolution. Something dark that exceeded the limits of simple lust and trespassed to a dangerous territory one didn't tread unless was ready to be altered by fire. Something I'd long missed and craved but would never have back. "When you read the whole thing, you'll know."

I don't like it when you talk to other men.

My gaze froze on the words. The only person who had said something like that to me was Tirone. He'd invaded my world, intoxicating me, with the same jealous possessiveness these words of another man— a dangerous criminal and a stranger—held. Laius Lazzarini was nothing but a potential threat I needed to address and a student I met a few weeks ago and was bound to leave after a few more. Yet I was so weak and desperate for a reminder, for something to fill the hole that was ripped out of my heart, that I didn't care about how inappropriate and ridiculous those words were or whom they came from.

Like an addict, I let them seep into my pores and give me a dark rapture, a fake euphoria that would numb the pain even for a few moments. With a warm sigh, I bit my lip on a smile.

Then it hit me. I might have made some decisions that truly questioned the level of my intelligence, and I was surely devastated enough to fill the void inside my chest with anything no matter how fake or Ludacris. But I wasn't that stupid.

While it sounded silly for a man to be jealous for a woman he'd barely spoken to or spent time with, a woman he hadn't touched or even seemed to like, it wasn't impossible. It'd happened to me before. Prior that day at the library, Tirone didn't exactly give me the easiest time in class. He was always mean and barely gave me any attention to the point I thought he hated me. It wasn't strange for me to see the same behavior from another student. A show of hate on the outside, quite the opposite on the inside.

But...not from Furore.

He was forty-one, not a teenager who had an unhealthy crush on the teacher. The president of the Night Skulls most certainly had had more than enough women at his disposal for years. Women that looked million times better than I did and were ready to please him in ways I didn't. I understood he was behind bars with no access to such entertainment, but he hadn't been here that long to lust over the fatback teacher—yes, I heard what they called me—let alone become jealous or possessive of me.

Furore was playing me, thinking he could get me to believe he had intimate feelings for me so I'd trust him enough to tell him another one of my secrets.

I grabbed the pencil from his hand and flipped it to erase his deceit, resolve to beat him in his own game coursing through me. "But you haven't even reached the minimum word limit. You only wrote two ridiculous lines. Write the whole thing, Laius. Stop caring about misspelling a few words and put more effort into writing down some in the first place."

He snatched the pencil back from my hand, touching my finger in the process, sending a wild turmoil of tingling need in me, shaking my resolve for a split-second, and wrote something else down. "How about now?"

Stop talking to that schmuck and I will finish the stupid assignment.

I'd do anything to get him to speak, even if it was leading him to believe he was successful with his manipulation. "Fine. I don't think that's very creative, but it's your assignment. I'll allow it."

He wrote something quickly. *Good girl.*

Despite myself, I twitched with a smile on my lips and a throb between my legs. What was it about those two words that floored us like that?

Fuck me for being that weak and depraved. "When you finish, you'll read for the class." And that was my *fuck you* to him.

He looked up at me as I straightened, surprise flicked in his eyes. Then he snorted a laugh. "No."

"That wasn't a request."

Still laughing, he hunched over the notebook and shrugged.

I threw a subtle glance at what he wrote next. *Take off your shades for me, and I'll think about it. I'm tired of imagining the eyes I look into when I fuck my fist every night. I wanna know what they look like for real.*

The crass expression penetrated my senses with fear and pleasure. A smirk curved his mouth as he lifted his eyes, taking his time with every curve of my body, darting the tip of his tongue and licking his lip. When he met my face, I was melting under his vulgar scrutiny.

Stop it. Don't let him win. It's all lies. He doesn't care about you. He just wants you to drop your guard, to come out from your hiding and be easy prey for whomever is hunting.

"You know this is giving me a headache." I set a hand on my hip and smiled at Murphy. "Maybe, I should have that coffee after all."

Furore cursed under his breath. Then he jumped to his feet. Reflexively, I took a step back. While he wasn't The Hulk, and his body and muscles weren't bulging—painfully proportional and sculpted but not humongous like those of Laniakea Kelekolio, for instance, Furore was much bigger than me and would easily take me down in a fight if it'd ever come to it. He was capable of hurting me. In many ways. He incited a certain fear in me that was far more powerful than that of physical strength. His energy was the most dominant I'd ever encountered, and the rage that was bubbling up under it was enough to sink my heart down to my knees.

Murphy came toward us. "Lazzarini, back to your seat."

Furore clenched one fist and with the other grabbed the notebook. For a second there, he looked like he was going to hit the guard with it. *Oh no*.

Murphy stood between me and Furore, pushing me back, clutching his baton. "Lazzarini, last warning."

I felt all eyes on us. A state of high alert filled the room. Any second now, this could turn into a riot in the classroom.

"Get out of the way." Furore's voice dripped with malice and threat.

"Back to your seat," Murphy said firmly, getting the baton out. "I won't say it again."

Furore shot him a death glare before he switched it toward me. "My teacher wants me to read for the class. I'm only respecting her wishes."

Finally, I could breathe. "Yes, Guard Murphy. I asked Laius to read his assignment to the class. Thank you, Laius. Please, head to the front," I said, even though the allocated time for finishing the assignment wasn't up. I didn't want any fights to disrupt my class. And strangely, I didn't want Laius to get hurt.

Murphy's tension didn't ease out, but he put the baton back in its place and escorted Furore and me to the front of the class.

Furore shot me a glance I understood without the need for words. I stood behind my desk and tilted so that my back was to Murphy and my attention solely was to Laius.

Just like the foreign feeling of fear for him and not of him that had snuck up on me and hadn't made any sense, an urge, despite the tension and fright of the situation, nagged me so irritatingly it couldn't be contained.

I gazed at him, and mouthed, "Good boy."

CHAPTER 8

FURORE

She's just a job. That bitch is just a fucking job.
Why the fuck was my blood simmering when she was talking to that pig? Why did I want to rip his dick off when she said she was gonna have coffee with him? Why did I truly want to see those eyes, for myself not for the Lanzas, and look right into them when I was balls deep inside her? Why did I want to shelter them, not expose them? Why did I want to keep the privilege of looking at them only mine?

Why was I standing here, making a fool of myself for her pleasure, only so she'd be looking at me, teasing me with words that put a silly grin on my face and made my cock jump?

"Why am I in this class?" I started. It wasn't to get distracted by a bitch. It wasn't to stir shit for her sake. It wasn't to get protective of her. It wasn't to get a motherfucking erection when she put her hair down and did that thing when she flipped it a little off her neck. It wasn't to want stupid things with her now or when I got out. A bitch like her didn't end up with motherfuckers like me. Motherfuckers like me didn't end up with a bitch like her. Didn't end up with any bitch. Period. It was time I was reminded why I was really in Miss Meneceo's class.

I opened my notebook and looked at the assignment I'd never written. The only words there were the ones that got her to blush that deep red that floored me. Making her uncomfortable, getting a rise out of her to see that redness to her cheeks was becoming the highlight of my week and my favorite source of entertainment.

"We're listening, Laius. Why are you here?" she said.

I snorted and snapped the notebook shut. "You know what? Fuck this shit."

"Excuse me?"

"I already told you why I'm here."

"But we'd like to hear it from you, in more elaborate words as you followed the instructions. Please read what you've written so far. It doesn't matter if it's perfect. What matters is that it's honest."

She knew I didn't write shit. She wanted honesty? Fine, I'd give her honesty. How hard could it be to give her a sob story a young girl like her would believe when my life had been a series of those for over forty years? Fuming, I opened the fucking thing and pretended to be reading. "In a life like mine, the most dangerous feeling you can get is fear. Whatever you do, you can't allow yourself to be afraid because the second it sneaks up on you, you lose." The first lesson I'd ever learned on the streets. "You have to be numb to fear. Everything you do, every ride, every rush, every drag, every pussy, it's all to push it down until it's no longer there."

Some inmates nodded their heads. Others just had those deep looks of the sorrow and pain we'd learned to bottle down inside on their faces. Jo was blushing again at my saying pussy, but she didn't dare scold me for it.

She'd pushed me into this shit. She didn't get to complain.

"With time, you convince yourself you're doing great," I continued. "You're the king of your own fucking world. You're even fucking happy. Because every second you live when you're not afraid, that's what happiness is. The only kind you know." I glanced up to the bars that separated me from everything I cared about. "Then you hold your baby for the first time, and you realize you've never been happy a day in your life. You've never been afraid a day in your life either. Because when I held my boy in my arms, I knew what it truly meant to feel both."

My gaze dropped back at her. "Bless your heart, Miss Meneceo, you wanna know why I'm here? I'm here in prison because I was protecting my boy. Even if his fucking bitch of a mom lied and framed me again, even if he didn't believe me, that's what I was doing. I'm here in your class because my son won't even talk to me. This shit you teach is the fucker's favorite subject. He's fucking brilliant at it. I thought, maybe, if I read the books he liked and learned how to write at his level, maybe, I could write him a letter good enough to get him to speak to me."

Again, I'd been distracted from my goal. I was supposed to feed her a sob story to make her trust me and loosen up, but I was the one here standing like a fucking idiot, with tears in his eyes. "After four weeks of education, I haven't gotten closer to my goal yet because he hasn't responded to any of my letters. The skills I've learned so far filled my head with other men's shit, got me insight into Shakespeare's and Hemmingway's heads, but not into my boy's. The difference I feel is that my hands are more fucking tied every second I'm here and he's out there, because I know he's been hearing nothing but more of the lies she's been poisoning him with, and he'll just keep on hating me. The measures I'll take to reach my goal?" I paused, sniffling. Then I wiped my face and nodded to myself. "Whatever it takes because what truly motivates me to keep going, and not just in the slammer but in life, is winning my boy back."

CHAPTER 9

JO

I wished I'd had a father like Laius. A man who wasn't afraid to go to prison, who would have protected his children at all costs. Who was ready to be better for their sake and did everything in his power to reunite with them.

Tears pricked my eyes as I listened, but I had my sunglasses to veil them from him and every other soul in here. However, when I saw his own tears, I was going to blubber ugly and didn't care what everyone would say.

But...just when I was about to lose all caution and fall for the sadness and pain behind his story, self-preservation kicked in. What if Furore was just as good as his son at the *shit* I taught? What if making up stories was a talent that ran in the family? What if this villain was trying to disguise himself in the tormented anti-hero cloak like he'd tried to sell me the jealous, possessive, student teacher crush narrative earlier? What if everything Furore had been doing to me since we'd met was a calculated measure to reach the real goal he was here for?

Fact check. Unlike the other students, he'd enrolled late in my class. It could be normal, but with his behavior, I was more inclined to believe otherwise. Perhaps he was never interested in taking my class or be better at writing to reach his son like he'd claimed. Perhaps he was ordered to take my class to have access to me. To discover the secrets very few people who lived knew. Had he not been trying to know things about me? He'd figured out I wasn't Italian, and today he was trying to get me to show my eyes.

Or I was being paranoid, everything he'd said about his son was true, he did want to see my eyes for his perverted reasons or to just win the notorious bet, and he was only riling me up about my identity to get me to lay off his back because I was an insufferable bitch.

Which theory was the truth?

"You happy?" Furore asked.

No. I was confused. My plan to get him to reveal his secret intentions hadn't satisfied me and left me needing more. "Thank you, Laius, for sharing your work. Disregarding all the swears, it was very good."

"Right on," he mocked and glanced at his peers. "Clap, motherfuckers."

They obeyed, erupting in whistles, cheers and applause. I snorted and gave a little smile. "Thank you, Laius! You can go back to your seat!"

He turned, giving Murphy a wink on his way back to the desk. Then he tossed the notebook on top of it and slumped down in his seat.

"Laius?" I asked when the class calmed.

"Yes, *Miss Meneceo*?"

I ignored the clench between my thighs every time he drawled my name in his mixed Italian Southern accent. "What's the name of your son?"

He stared at me for a second, taken aback. Then his gaze held my face steadily. "Rex."

Rex? Was I supposed to believe that? Assuming that wasn't a name you gave a dog rather than your own son, had he not lectured me about the Italian alphabet before? Had he not assumed I checked and knew by now what letters it had? Because I had, and x, just like j, wasn't included.

How stupid do you think I am, Furore?

"Well, I sincerely hope your time here can be of help to reconnect with *Rex*. I have no doubt you can excel in Creative Writing. Your paragraph while crude is very impressive." I switched my gaze to the rest of the students, anger coursing under my skin. "What your classmate did here wasn't just an assignment. He succeeded at using the main pillar of every story out there to make you believe him. He grasped the fundamentals of building a character and outlined our course for us."

I wrote three letters on the board, hitting hard on the marker, pouring my frustration into a learning experience. How fucking professional of me. *GMC*. "Goal, motivation and conflict." I spun and stared at Furore. My student with the accent that made me wet and the eyes that commanded my forbidden orgasms. And my new enemy. "No matter how fictitious or unbelievable your story is, build a character using these three, then give it the right depth with a sad backstory, you'll have every reader around your finger. They'll believe and even crave your lies, shed tears for your pain and clap for your talent. That is what constitutes great fiction. It's magical, isn't it? But at the end of the day, it's just another lie."

CHAPTER 10

FURORE

One Week Ago

"Tell me you got something," I said the second I sat at the table.

"Not even I miss you, bro?" Fort, my Road Captain, grinned in a tease.

"*I miss you, bro.* Now fucking speak."

He sighed, losing his grin. He ran a hand through his long, jet black hair, and his thick eyebrows furrowed before he clasped his hands and leaned forward. "I've set all our crew and prospects to listen to every whistle and whisper out there."

I threw a hand in the air in exasperation. Patience hadn't been my friend in weeks, and now it was taking its last breath. "And?"

"Look, you were right about the Italian honeymoon. It's over. The Lanza-Bellomo alliance is no more."

"C'mon, Fort. Give me something I don't know. Something I can work with."

"It looks like the Bellomos are gaining turf. They now own Kentucky and Michigan, not just Chicago, and the Irish up north are getting in bed with them. Tino Bellomo is expanding his empire fast, and everybody is game, even the MCs. He has the Wicked Warriors on his side."

"So the Lanzas need to expand, too, to counter his move. They can't rely just on the West. But why the South when it's the hardest to slip in? Why not go east?"

Fort leaned closer, lowering his voice. "There are rumors Bellomo is planning on taking that, too. He's already talking with the Italians there, but the only problem is, he has serious beef with the Irish in Boston and New York. They'll never let him in."

"The Larvins?" I matched his whisper.

He nodded. "That means one thing. The enemy of my enemy…"

"The Lanzas are getting in bed with them to gain turf in the East. Together they'll be strong enough to match the Bellomos. Then they'll come to steal our turf before the Bellomos try to do the same. Fuck."

"Well, the good news is, Tino Bellomo isn't a greedy motherfucker. He's batshit crazy, but he's like elite and territorial as fuck. He protects what he has, and I don't reckon he's stupid enough to waste it on a useless war in the South. The Italian Mafia has tried for years to get on our land, but it always ends in loss of money and blood. We're immune, bro. Texas is a fucking fort, like me." He laughed, his big body shaking with humor I couldn't share.

"The Lanzas look desperate enough to try something as stupid as going to *a useless war*."

"But I have more good news. The Larvins don't like the Lanzas either. They don't give a shit about an alliance. Without the fucking Irish, the Lanzas can't do squat. They can go *fanculo*."

I hooked my hands behind my head and put the pieces together. Then a dreadful memory filled my throat with bile. "Shit."

"Why shit? Ease up, brother. This is good news. They can't do shit."

"No." I whispered. "They can do a lot if she is who they think she is."

He grinned. "The hot teach?"

My jaws clenched hard. I didn't like anyone saying anything about her body, not even my best friend. "Fifteen years ago, Declan Larvin had a bastard kid for eight years in the dark. When the wife found out, she sent men to kill the switch on the mother and the kid together. The fucker let her as if that wasn't his blood she was spilling. The girl's mother died, and they said the kid met the same destiny, but word on the street, there was only one grave dug that fit a grown bitch, not an eight-year-old."

He pursed his lips, contemplating. "If the teach is Larvin's girl…"

"The Lanzas will serve her on a silver platter to the Larvins. They get the allies they need, and with our help, which they'll get as long as they have me by the fucking balls, they find a way with the MCs in Texas. The war to come won't be as useless as you think."

"Fuck. Is she the kid?"

"I don't know yet, but…" My gut told me she wasn't just *not* Italian. She was hiding something big. She wore a fucking wig in the summer for fuck's sake. I could tell that wasn't her hair because when my sister got cancer she sent me to buy her wigs. She taught me how to pick them, to spot the synthetic from the real and to choose the ones that looked the least fake. She gave me shit when I bought the ones with bad hairlines. It was always about the fucking hairline. Jo's wig, for those who never bought one before, looked as real as it got. For me, I could spot the treacherous little light roots on her cream white forehead. She was fucking blonde, and with every day that passed, I was more willing to bet my own dick on Irish eyes.

"You gotta give the dog a bone. Do whatever it takes to get outta here, and the rest can be taken care of. Supported by the Irish or not, we'll make sure they never set foot in our territory." He shrugged. "Larvin's kid or just a teach with bad luck, just give her to them."

"No," I said fast.

"No? They're gonna pull the plug on your boy's shitty stepdad. Your ass will rot in here for four fucking years instead of two if not more."

"I'm not gonna let them touch her," I gritted under my breath.

He shook his head, pulling at the back of his hair. "It's your call, Prez, but squander it all for some pussy? You? I've never seen you like this, Furore. Your brothers need ya more than ya need that pussy. Your boy needs ya. "

"You think I don't know that?" I growled. "But I'm not gonna let them lay a hand on her, you hear me?" I wouldn't let *anybody* hurt her. Not anymore.

He shrugged, putting his hands out in surrender. "Gonna tell me why?"

I just stared at him. I didn't have a straight answer to tell my Road Captain or even myself. She wasn't mine to protect, not my child, not my pussy, not my blood. But even if I had yet to feel her clench and cream around my cock, I just knew I had to keep her safe as if she was mine. Until I made her mine.

And if she was Larvin's lost kid, if she was Madeline's daughter, then I owed her a lot more than just protection.

"Wow." He chuckled. "How big is that ass?"

"Fuck you, Fort."

"All right, all right. But please tell me you have another plan to get outta this dump. I ain't spending the next four years taking eighteen-hour rides to this funk ass town every weekend to visit your old ass."

He was right. I had to get out of here as fast as possible. For my boy. For my brothers and the MC. And for her. "Here's what we're gonna do."

CHAPTER 11

JO

Belle View club was one of the most beautiful upscale places in San Francisco. Vibrant and had a big square bar with blue and magenta neon light straps in the counter body. Packed with people, the sound of laughter, good music and sex. Around every dark corner, there were heels hooked around hips accompanied by moans and grunts. A happy, care-free place for happy, care-free people.

I wasn't one of those people, so I contemplated leaving at least ten times in the past fifteen minutes I'd been here. Coming tonight wasn't even my idea. It was Perla's. The P.E. teacher at the school. She'd called me and every female teacher that was doing the summer courses for a girl's night out. *No one should spend the summer with flunking teens in the morning and grading papers in the evening. So take off your underwear and meet me at Belle View. Your vagina needs air. Also tequila and a fat cock.* Her words, not mine.

It was more than odd for me to accept the invitation. I never went anywhere. I always kept to myself. Someone with so many secrets to hide and protect had to. But I needed company tonight. I was tired of the ghosts that haunted my nights, dead and living. I needed a distraction, something, anything to keep my mind off Ty and the horrendous past. After the latest class at San Quentin, the recent distraction I'd been using had turned into a source of pain as well.

What did I expect? An honest criminal? A convict with honor and respect? Of course, he was a liar. Men like Furore said and did anything to get what they wanted no matter the consequences. They didn't care what or whom they hurt or manipulate along the way. *They don't give a shit.* I'd learned that the hard way. Why, for the love of God, just to get over a boy, had I allowed myself to get attached to a stupid fantasy when I knew it'd lead to no good?

And now that I was pretty sure Furore had an ulterior motive joining my class—this couldn't be just about winning a bet—boy problems were the least of my worries.

What was he gaining from getting closer to me? Was he trying to find out whom I really was for him or for someone else?

The Cosmo I gulped didn't warm the ice pit in my stomach. The idea of just packing my little, lonely, pathetic life and go start over somewhere else sounded more than tempting. I had nothing here to risk being found for…except a false hope my ratchet heart still clung to.

"Jo! C'mon, girl! Tell us what you think!" Perla yelled over the music.

I frowned. I hadn't been listening to a word she, Laura, the Physics teacher, and Christine, the History teacher were saying. "About what?"

She feigned shock, putting a hand on her chest, eyes bulging. Then she, not so subtly, pointed at the bar where a man in a white T-shirt and a leather vest—a cut?—with full sleeves of tattoos on his bulging arms sat, downing shots. "If you don't go, I will!"

"Go where?"

"Talk to him. See if he's interested." She giggled.

"Oh! No." I shook my head rapidly. "You, by all means, have at it."

"You shittin' me? Have you looked at him? And the emblem on his cut?"

I narrowed my eyes to take a closer look. Our table was at the back, distant from lurking eyes, and I'd chosen the least visible seat to the bar. I couldn't make the emblem from here.

"Take off the ugly shades, girl, to get a better look," Christine said.

I pushed them up my nose, as if they were going to fall off, holding on to them more. "I'm photophobic. My eyes are very sensitive. The strobe lights will kill me."

"That's the emblem of the Night Skulls MC." Perla saved me. "Ever heard of them?"

More than I should have. I just nodded.

"I think they used to own this place. They threw the wildest of parties at their compound." She spoke about them as if they were gods. She didn't know they were lying thugs that used and hurt people. "Back in college, I met one of them here. He took me to one of their parties at Rosewood and we…" She uttered strange sounds that were supposed to refer to sex. "His name is Dusty, and he is, hands down, the best I've ever had."

"Oh my God." Laura put down her drink. "Isn't that their young hot president that took over when his father died?"

Perla nodded emphatically, sipping her cocktail.

"Fuck, I envy you, you dirty, dirty slut."

"Isn't he dead?" I blurted out.

They stared at me, their laughter deceased. Well, if it weren't me to be the party pooper and kill the mood…

"I mean, they said the fire killed them all, but what do I know?" I pointed at the bulky man at the bar in an attempt to lighten up the conversation. "Which chapter?"

"Huh?" Perla hummed.

"The Night Skulls have chapters, like groups, all over the world. They're global. Which chapter does he belong to?"

Christine grinned. "All knowledgeable about chapters and bikers and shit? Wait a second. Do you have bikers in your class in prison? OMG, you totally do, don't you? That's why you're not interested in that guy. You have another at your disposal, don't you, Miss Meneceo?" She made the last sentence sound dirty.

My eyebrows shot high. "I…um…as a matter of fact, some of the students are affiliated, yes."

Perla gasped. "Do tell."

"There's nothing to tell. They are not as hot as you think they are." I scratched my neck at the blatant lie. "What makes you think I'll be interested in a biker anyway?"

"Maybe you're not, but your vagina is."

"She told you that over the phone?"

She laughed at my snarky joke, most likely because she was tipsy. Nobody laughed at my jokes. "She doesn't need to. Every vagina is interested in a biker."

There was a time when my heart leapt and my sex clenched every time I heard a motorcycle roar. Ty rode a bike everywhere, even to school. While his father was a member of the Night Skulls here—and died in that fire—Ty never belonged to an MC or had a cut, but he rocked leather jackets and rode like he did. There was nothing that took the edge off for me like when we used to meet outside of San Francisco—so no one we knew would see us—and he took me on his motorcycle and rode for hours across California.

Now, the mention of bikers brought heartache, and every bike I saw was disappointed anticipation followed by squashed hope because Tirone wasn't on it. "Well, mine needs to do something more vital and far less attractive. Excuse me, ladies. I'm glad Mrs. Williams isn't here."

Their giggles followed me as I made my way to the bathroom. After I was done, I decided I'd stay for one more drink and then go home. I was a fish out of water here, taking a part in a scene I only read about in books. Talking to some stranger in order to hopefully get picked up at a bar was never my plan. I was only here for the booze that would make me tired enough to go straight to bed. But the girls seemed to have other plans, and I had no intention to be included in them.

They were still talking boys when I returned, shooting gazes at the mystical biker, willing him to look their way, but he never turned his head.

"Do you remember that sophomore kid that rode a Harley to school? That boy is yummy."

Laura was talking to Perla, but it was me who responded, my heart eaten in flames of rage and jealousy. "Wisely. His name is Tirone Wisely. Should we really be talking about students like that?" They shouldn't be talking about him like he was a piece of meat. They shouldn't be talking about him at all.

"C'mon. No one is listening," Perla laughed. "Besides, he doesn't go to our school anymore."

"They say he's slept with the entire class within five weeks. The fuck?"

"Can you blame them? He's so gorgeous. Another few years, and I'd happily let him spread my legs and eat—"

"I'm going to get some air!" I said, louder than I should have. "It's getting too hot in here." I moved as fast as I could away from the table, and then tears wet my lashes.

The humid air hit my skin as I tried to even my breath. It felt like my lungs were going to crash and my heart was going to burst. It wasn't the first time I'd heard women or girls talk about how sexy Ty was or the things they'd let him do to them. It wasn't the first time I had to eat shit, keep my mouth shut about it and act like I wasn't jealous or hurt over it. It was one of the many prices I was paying for being in a secret, forbidden relationship, but tonight I couldn't bear it anymore.

I came here to get my mind off things, off him, for once, but this night kept getting worse. God, I wished I'd smoked. I needed to burn something instead of burning myself.

My eyes rolled heavenwards. "When will it end? All the pain and fear and loneliness, when will it end?"

I wiped under my eyes, convinced I should cancel that last drink and go home now before the night got any worse. Storming inside, I didn't reach the door before I hit a human tank. It was the MC guy the girls were horny for. I didn't know what he was built of, but it wasn't flesh and bones like the rest of ordinary humans. His chest was so solid I felt as if I hit an unmovable surface. An exasperated huff streamed out of my lungs as I held my hands out in a rough apology.

"It's my bad, doll. Had too many in there," he drawled in a Southern accent, chuckled and went on his way.

Southern accent? Night Skulls cut? Did he know Furore?

I stood there for a few moments, following him with my gaze. His cut only said Texas. Should I ask him if he was from Houston? Should I just ask straight if he knew Furore?

What if he did? Who cared if a random man I met at a bar knew him? What would that piece of information be of any good to me? I shouldn't care about bad Laius

Lazzarini in any way whatsoever. Not even as a student because he never really wanted to be.

But what were the odds of having a Night Skull from Texas at a San Francisco bar on the night I was in?

Before my head rambled any further, the biker straddled his motorcycle and another pulled over by his side at the parking lot. My eyes tightened at the newcomer. I recognized that helmet.

Taking a closer look at the Harley, I gasped silently. As the biker took off his helmet, and his dark brown hair fell off his forehead, my heart skipped a beat.

"Ty," I slurred, shuddering. "H-how?"

My head spun with the shock and vodka. I thought he'd left San Francisco. I thought he'd taken off with his family. But he was here. All this time, Tirone was in the city, and he didn't even bother saying anything.

"What the fuck?" I hiccupped through the tears.

He wasn't injured or sick or anything. He was smiling and talking to the other biker without a care in the world. "How? How could he just…?"

He forgot all about me just like that. He tossed me away like a whore he was done with. Even worse. At least, whores got paid for their services. Perhaps, they got a goodbye every now and then, too. I wasn't even worthy of that. I was nothing to him when he was everything to me.

Shaking with more tears, I spun, wishing I'd been dead. I was supposed to be fifteen years ago, but I fucking lived. For what?

Go talk to him. He must have an explanation.

No. I wouldn't make any more excuses for him. He had months to reach out and explain, but he didn't. He chose to leave in that disgusting way. What was left to explain?

I moaned in silence as I dragged myself back in, thankful for the sunglasses that hid my pain from the world. Not that I cared anymore. Let them see. Let them know. Let them fucking find me and end my pitiful life.

But no. I'd live. I'd find a way to forgive myself and start over. No one was worth destroying myself. I'd survived for twenty-three years. I'd survive some more because I wouldn't let any of those fucking bad guys win.

I grabbed my purse and headed out with one thought in my head. I had to leave and never come back. Nothing tied me to this city anymore. A clean slate was in order. For that to happen, there was something I had to do first at San Quentin.

CHAPTER 12

JO

"Good afternoon, everyone," I said as my inmate students took their seats. I didn't bother greeting them one by one, each by their name, to maintain the rapport I strived to create. There was no point anymore.

"Hey, Miss Jo," Laniakea answered with a huge yawn. Then he stopped in his tracks when his stare landed on my outfit. I wasn't in my regular suit today. A pink, knee-length, summer skirt and a white blouse replaced it. "May I say how nice you look today?"

"Thanks."

He smiled wryly. "Special occasion?"

My final act before I disappeared. My farewell gift. Besides, if they were fucking their filthy fists to me anyway, I might as well choose how I looked when they did.

"Take a seat, Laniakea, please."

"Ohhhh, someone is going on a date," he teased, seating his huge body on the chair that barely fit him. I gave him a warning gaze until he wiped that grin off his face.

"A date? What fucking date?" Connor, an all bark no bite student, asked with a frown. "C'mon, Miss M. you're breaking my heart."

I was in no mood for any silly banter, so ignoring him, I rolled my eyes toward my desk. That was when I clashed with Furore's smoldering gaze. He looked at me as if he was going to kill me, but not before he fucked me with his eyes. My whole body flushed under his inappropriate gaze.

"Answer the man. What fucking date?" he seethed.

Why the hell did he care whether I dated or not? Did he still think I was buying whatever he was trying to pull off to get what he needed to know about me? *Drop the fucking act, Furore. The game is over. You lost.*

"Get. To. Your. Seat." I yanked my gaze and darted it at the rest of the students. "Everybody. Now."

Furore's stare snapped at me, flickering with fire. I pressed my mouth into a hard line, daring him to defy me.

He twined his fingers together and moved them inward and upward with pop sounds, as if he was getting ready for a fist fight. Whom was he going to beat almost to death? He wouldn't dare come near me here. Right?

He switched his stare toward Murphy. "You going out with the guard? Prison teacher and guard, how fucking fitting. You read that trope in one of your cheesy porn books and thought why not try it yourself?"

"Lazzarini, zip it and take a seat," Murphy said in warning.

Furore slammed the desk surface as he sat down, glaring menacingly at Murphy.

I was sick of his bullshit. "You don't know the kind of books I read, but even *cheesy porn* books with that trope are much better than others like, let's say, prison teacher and inmate." They usually ended up with him using her to break out of jail or giving her as payment to whomever helped.

"Davvero? Why, Miss Meneceo? I bet the inmate can last longer than the guard, make the teacher come much harder. Several times."

"That's it!" Murphy dashed toward Furore, baton in hand.

Panic jolted through me. Furore was an asshole who wouldn't give a shit about anyone but himself, but he, fake student or not, was still my responsibility. I didn't want him to get hurt. Not with a freaking baton that could smash his bones. My fists clenched as I darted to stand between the two of them. "HEY!"

Rendered speechless, everyone stared at me as my yell ricocheted around them. Murphy, who pushed me to his side to shield me from whatever shit that was about to hit the fan, blinked in disbelief. "Step back, Miss Meneceo."

"No," I dared. "I can handle it on my own. I didn't ask for your help."

Anger flashed on his face. "This is a prison, ma'am. I don't wait for you to ask for help to maintain order."

"It's my classroom. I—"

The door flew open, and the warden stormed in. "What the hell is going on here?" he roared.

Murphy opened his mouth, but I spoke first. "Just a discussion that led to a differing of literary opinion. Nothing to worry about.

It's all fine now. Right, Laius?" I leveled a look that demanded obedience at Furore.

He nodded sharply, still shooting dirty looks at Murphy.

"It didn't sound like nothing." The warden eyed the room, throwing a pointed stare at each inmate until he seemed satisfied they were under control. "I'd like to bring in your new student." He turned his head toward the door. "Maverick."

CHAPTER 13

FURORE

*S*on *of a fucking bitch.*

"With all due respect, Warden Mathews, the class is full, and we've covered, at least, one third of the curriculum I've prepared already. This unplanned addition won't be fair to the new student or the old," Jo told the fucking warden. The Lanzas must have fucking bought him to bring this dipshit in here.

I didn't need this shit today. I came here to find her in a motherfucking skirt, showing these pieces of shit more of herself than she'd ever offered, a hint of what she was saving for a fucking pompous ass like Murphy. Already, I'd been fuming with fury all week because she thought I was lying to her about my son.

I wasn't. Every word I said was true, and it messed up my head that she didn't believe me. The first time I opened up about my issues with my boy, and I was called a liar. Why I thought she, of all people, would see behind the walls that surrounded me and sift the truth from my words was an act of madness, but I did. I hoped for it. I wanted her to know that side of me. If I was being honest, I wanted her to know all of me. I wanted to lie bare, tell her about every sin, every crime, every flaw, every need so she could see me, hoping against all hope she'd still like me. It was selfish of me to want her to like me when I'd been sent to her own domain to destroy it. To destroy her.

She wasn't a dumb, little girl. She knew I was on to her, *using her to break out of jail or giving her as payment to whomever helped.*

She had to know I changed my mind. From the first time I laid eyes on her, a protective urge of her spurted out of nowhere, sending all my instincts on haywire. I wasn't gonna hurt her. Madeline's girl or not, I wasn't gonna hurt her.

The Lanzas must have sniffed something about it because they'd sent their bitch over to do the job I'd been stalling to finish. All I needed was some more time to get Fort to go on with my new plan, and then I'd have been out of here where I'd have been free of their threats. Where I could have protected my boy and her.

"Maverick has shown good progress with the other teachers. I'm sure he can keep up," Warden Fuckbitch said, and I wanted to rip his throat.

"Fine. Whatever," she said with a displeased sigh and gestured at Maverick to enter. "Have a seat."

No, Jo. Why didn't she fight harder? Like she fought for her authority a second ago when the pig was coming for me? *Or do you only do it when it's about me, baby?*

I'd have been flattered and fucking happy for the first time in months if it hadn't been for that Maverick dick, winking at me with a shit-eating grin as he stuck his motherfucking foot in the classroom.

She held a book and started handing out last week's papers back to us, red notes decorating them. As much as I wanted to read what she had to say about mine, my whole focus was on Maverick. I knew why he was here. To get her to take off her shades. A thick fuck like him could only do it by a stupid trick or a violent one. If he came near her, my ass would flip. I had to do something. I wouldn't let his dirty hands on her or let him confirm the Lanzas' suspicions about her.

"We're not discussing anything new today," she said, walking among desks, eyes lusting over her legs and ass the second she turned. I glared and snarled at every motherfucker I caught, and they quickly averted their gazes. Except for that fucker Maverick.

I wasn't a jealous man in the core, but only because I didn't give enough shit about just one pussy. The sweetbutts lined up at the club on display for all of the brothers, who knew never to touch anything I was interested in. Not until I was done. I hadn't had to mark my territory in ages. I'd already claimed my turf and kept it for years. No one dared take as much as a glance at it. But with Jo, it was different. I was different. "We're revising what we've learned so far. I want to make sure you've fully grasped—"

"You're so fine. Like *fine* fine," Maverick interrupted, and I clenched my fists so hard my knuckles were white.

She cocked a brow at him. "Using fine three times in two consecutive phrases? I'm not sure what other classes you've been taking where you've shown *good progress* in, but Creative Writing or anything related to language, obviously, isn't one. I understand you're new here, but what you said is both redundant and inappropriate. I'm your teacher. It's common sense that you don't say things like that to your teacher, understood?"

He fucking grinned, not taking his stare off her. "I bet you'll look even prettier without your shades on. Show me your eyes, baby."

I'm gonna punch the shit of that slimy mob bitch. I lifted my ass off the chair, but she was quicker than me. She took the book she was holding and smacked him on the back of his head with it. "I said this is inappropriate."

Laughter barked while the piece of shit swore. The guard was marching toward him as several other students rose to their feet. A smile broke on my face. A strange sense of pride filled me as she lashed out at him. *Baby girl got a spine.*

"Sorry." Maverick lifted his hands in surrender like the coward he'd always been when he saw Murphy. "I just really wanna see your eyes."

She stepped away, her forehead wrinkled and red, but the mob bitch stood and yelled, "Hey, I'm talking to you. Don't turn your back on me, bitch." In a split-second, his arm stretched to her shoulder, grabbing her and spinning her in his direction. I flew off my chair, ready to break his fucking bones. Jaw hung low, she gasped as his hand reached for her shades. The motherfucking prick was going to take them off her face.

My elbow collided with his jaw as I shielded her body away from his, and then I bent his arm until it snapped. Everything was happening so fast and loud. His screams and hers fueled the adrenaline pumping through my veins. As I was about to swoop down on the fucker, pain cracked in my back and behind my knees. Murphy's fucking baton.

I fell to my knees with a growl before I was grabbed and hurled against the wall. My gaze sought after her as I was being cuffed with one question in my head. Did that son of a bitch Maverick get to her? Did he manage to take the shades off her face?

CHAPTER 14

JO

Everyone was on their feet. More guards dashed into the room—Murphy must have hit the panic alarm to summon them—as he was lunging at Laius with his baton, and not the asshole who tried to grab me.

"Hey!" I shouted as Murphy pushed and pummeled Laius hard while cuffing him. "He was trying to protect me."

"He was disturbing the environment with aggravated violence."

"And what are you doing, huh?"

"Keeping him in check, ma'am."

I jabbed a finger at Maverick, who was now cuffed against the wall by the other guards. "*That* inmate is the one who tried to grab me. Laius was trying to protect me. Whatever you're doing to him is unnecessary." And fucking vindictive.

"Oh, Miss Meneceo, it's very necessary," Murphy countered with a harsh voice, twisting Laius's arm with a sadistic smile.

I flinched at Laius's cry out in pain. "Hey!" I stormed over to the rabble of angry men. Laius, cheek pressed into the wall, barely shook his head at me, as if begging me not to interfere. I scowled at the asshole I'd considered cute once and thought I might go out with. "I saw that! Get the warden here. Now."

"I don't work for you, ma'am. You know where his office is." He pulled Laius away from the wall, and blood was trailing from Laius's forehead down his eyebrow.

"He's bleeding!"

"He's fine," Murphy barked. He hauled Laius away toward the door but was halted by my firm, unmoving hand on his chest.

"Wait," I gritted and pulled a tissue out of the pack in my pocket. Then I moved it to Laius's forehead.

His face read different things. The obvious were the surprise and confusion that mirrored mine. It didn't take a genius to know the new student was only here for the purpose Laius seemed to have failed to serve for no reason I could fathom.

Why did he protect me?

Why could I not stand the brutality he'd faced to defend me? Why did his shout of pain squeeze around my heart? Why did I care if Laius Lazzarini was beaten or bleeding? Why did it hurt that his pain was caused by me?

As I carefully swiped the blood, his stare pierced me. "You don't need to—"

"Shut up and let me help you," I bit.

The finality in my voice shut his mouth with a snap. He took a deep breath, his gaze leaving a warm trail from my cheeks to my chest. My heart banged against my ribs as I felt every movement he made while I touched his face, every heated breath that whispered his own secrets across my palm.

I swallowed, unspoken words and questions swirling between us. Every time his mouth twitched near the frantic pulse in my wrist, my breath hitched. How would it feel to have his lips on my skin, right on top of my pulse where he could feel how much of a mess he was making me?

After I wiped all the blood, I stared intently around his face, buying all the time I could have with him. I was probably never going to see him again. It was for the best yet it made me dizzy with inexplicable pain.

A mark appearing on his forehead distracted me for a second. The urge to touch it left me in disarray. I wanted to ease the redness through my fingertips to soothe the pain it must have been causing him. I wanted to kiss it away. I wanted to kiss him. On his beautiful lips. On every part of his sculpted glory.

But I couldn't. Even if, by his now smoldering gaze on my lips, he seemed to share the same desires.

"I'm done," I muttered, wiping a spot of blood on my thumb, "but before you go, I want you to see something." I looked around the classroom. "All of you."

I moved back to my desk so everyone could see. Then I took off my sunglasses.

As what seemed to have been a hundred pairs of eyes fixed on me, gasps flew, followed by swear words in multiple languages I didn't need to master to identify. Maverick cursed louder than the others. Shocked or disappointed?

Who cared? This was my last class, and tomorrow I'd no longer be in San Francisco. Giving everybody the answer they needed was the one thing I had to do to ensure my safety as I started over. But I was curious about one thing.

I pinned my stare to Furore. "Did you win…or lose?"

He frowned. He opened his mouth, but no words came. Then he scoffed before the guards marched him out of the classroom.

CHAPTER 15

JO

"Excuse me, you're what?" The warden scowled at me behind his desk, a vein popping in his wide forehead.

"Leaving," I stressed.

"You can't leave in the middle of the semester without prior notice."

"I volunteer here, Mr. Mathews. I'm not obligated by anything other than my will and care for the students' educational welfare to stay. After what happened today, though, I'm no longer willing to take any risks, for anybody."

"Your safety isn't something we take lightly, Miss Meneceo, and I understand you had an *issue* with Murphy today. I'll replace him with not one but two guards."

I didn't know I was that important of an employee at San Quentin. I fought the urge to snort. He'd allowed a new student in my classroom when it was already full and almost half the semester had passed. At the first few minutes of Maverick's existence in my class, he was trying to grab my sunglasses off my face. Coincidence? Highly unlikely. Now, the warden was taking extra measures to keep me here. Obvious much?

I rose to my feet so he'd understand I wasn't willing to negotiate. I wasn't that stupid. "Did you bet, too?"

He touched his mustache like some villain in a black and white movie. "On what?"

I chuckled. "You know what."

"I'm not a gambling man, Miss Meneceo. I hate losing. But there isn't much to do around here for entertainment, so..." He shrugged.

"What color did you bet on? Let me guess. Green? No. Probably blue."

A smirk curved the corner of his thin lips. "Hazel."

"Wow." I didn't expect that. "You're a very lucky man. How much did you win?"

He looked me straight in my eyes—in my hazel contacts. "About five hundred dollars."

"Well, I hope you put them in good use. Perhaps to put on an ad to find someone to fill my place." I carried my things and drove straight to my apartment. I had a lot of packing to do.

A motorcycle engine revved next to my car as I arrived at the apartment building. My shameless heart careened, and my eyes widened at the window to catch a glimpse of the motorcycle…or the rider. It dashed right by me, though. In a flash it was a dot at the end of the dark street before it vanished completely.

My shoulders slumped as I shook my head at the tightening in my chest. Why did I keep doing this to myself? Tirone had forgotten about me, and I'd made up my mind to go. He didn't deserve the torture I was inflicting upon myself. He didn't deserve to live rent-free in my mind and heart, branding his name on my soul with fire.

I grabbed my bag and headed to the building entrance. Then I looked for my keys. Tonight, it all ended. No more Tirone, no more—

Something rough covered my mouth and stifled my scream. "No, no!" My voice came out muffled. I squirmed, fighting as hard as I could.

"Don't move. Just open the door and get in," an unfamiliar, gruff, male voice said.

I could see the beefy hand on my mouth now, and it pressed harder to silence my cries. It got harder to breathe and with that my muscles didn't cooperate to execute any moves to defend myself. Tears streamed down my face, and fear sucked the blood out of my body. They found me. I was a few hours away from leaving town, but they fucking found me. How?

"Now," he growled.

With shaky hands, I unlocked the door. He pushed me in fast and closed the door right behind us.

"Please, let me go," I sniffled in the dark against his palm, writhing in the ironclad arms that wouldn't budge, choking.

"Don't fight. Lead us up to your place."

"No."

His arm became a tight hold on my throat, and I discovered his hand on my mouth was nothing. I knew now what it meant to be really choking. "Don't make me hurt you," he said, dragging me toward the stairs.

He was so big, practically lifting me off my feet when I still wouldn't obey him, as he took us both upstairs. He released my throat only to take my keys and after several tries unlock the door to my apartment.

Once we were inside, he turned on the lights. "Now, I'm gonna take my hand off your mouth, and you'll be a good bitch and not scream."

"Fuck you," I huffed, but I didn't think it was clear enough.

"We can do this the easy way or the hard way. Either way, you'll fucking listen to what I have to say."

I grimaced in confusion, suddenly registering his accent. Southern. And on a second thought, it wasn't that unfamiliar. "Who are you?"

"What's that, babe?"

"Who are you?!"

"You gonna behave?"

Reluctantly, I nodded. I was going to suffocate anyway if he didn't take his hand off my mouth.

Slowly, his grip eased off me, and the constriction in my lungs started to lift. I twisted to see his face. "What... I know you. You're the biker from the club. What are you doing here and what do you want from me?"

CHAPTER 16

FURORE

I could have bet my own soul she was Madeline's kid. She got her spine...and ass. Those hazel eyes, though...

Part of me wanted it to be Madeline's daughter so I could do right by the one woman I should have never left twenty-five years ago. A frustrated, yet relieved, sigh blew out of me. At least, they weren't gonna kill her. At least, when I got out, I could make her mine without having to look over my shoulder every second to protect her.

Picturing the hazel eyes, I spat on my hand and wrapped it around my dick in the darkness of the hole. I got solitary for one fucking week for *hitting the teacher.* Those fuckers. Mathews was definitely on the Lanzas' payroll. I was being punished for not doing the job they'd sent me to do, for defending Jo instead of giving her to them, even when she turned out to be not the girl they were looking for.

That meant one thing. She wasn't out of the danger zone. I, like a stupid fuck, had just put a target on her back when I defended her. I couldn't risk it. How was I supposed to know she wasn't the Larvin's daughter? I should have stepped back, but even if I'd known she wasn't the lost Irish bastard, I wouldn't have just stood by and watched. I couldn't just let him touch her. The thought alone simmered my blood and then rushed it down to my cock, like I were an animal that had to mark his territory, ready to claim its mate.

I licked my lip as I pictured her bent over her desk while I pushed hard inside her wet pussy and watched her ass as my cock slipped in and out of her. Like I'd been doing for weeks. This time, though, I took off her wig and wrapped her real hair around my wrist. Then I pulled and forced her hazel eyes to look at me while they darkened and rolled back at me. "The only hands that will worship your body are gonna be mine. The only cock that will fuck you until you see heaven is my cock, baby girl. God, I wanna fuck you so hard."

Undressing her until her tits spilled on my chest and her ass was filling my grip, imagining the sweet moans and begs that would come out of her lips, I rubbed faster, harder.

Laius. My balls tightened as her voice rasped my name in my head. Then my cum spilled out, thick and hot, covering the back of my hand, the tip of my cock and sliding down the shaft. I pictured her licking it all off, and I was hard all over again.

Maybe, I should go one more time. Two times in a row would help knock me out so I'd stop worrying about what might happen. The Lanzas wouldn't stop pursuing their greed. They must have known by now I cared about her. They could still use her against me to get what they wanted. They could use my boy, too.

That was why I'd sent Fort to watch over them and send them both messages, hoping they'd listen.

Fuck, I wished I hadn't been locked in a goddamn hole for a week with no means of communication with the outside world. I needed to know if Fort came through with the plan that would get me out of here, and I needed to know if Jo and my boy were safe.

The meal slot opened, and light burst into the darkness. It took my gaze and ears a minute to adjust to the light and the noise the plate was making. Then a huge pair of eyes stared at me that belonged more to a lemur rather than a human, but they did belong to a guard named Landor. He wasn't a total asshole.

"You didn't hear this from me, but your ass is getting out of here, Furore," he said.

"Out of the hole?"

"Out of the Arena. Your wife changed her testimony. The charge will be dropped soon enough. *Bless your heart*, you're one lucky motherfucker."

I bolted upright, ignoring the offensive sarcasm. I didn't say he was great. He was still a pig. "I'm being released?"

"Yup."

"Thank fuck." Finally, I was getting out of this shit hole. Finally, I got to protect the people I loved and cared about. My family and Jo.

"And one more thing, the teacher left."

"Left?"

"She's not coming back. They're saying she's skipping town, too."

The relief I was basking in a second ago shattered in pieces. "What?"

"That's what they're saying."

No. This can't be happening. She can't just leave. That couldn't be the last time I saw her. I have to see her again. I have to make sure she's safe. She has to listen to me and let me explain. How could she leave just like that? Fuck. "When are they gonna get me out of the hole?"

"Don't know, but it's earlier than a week. You should be grateful. Eat your dinner, count your fucking blessings and get your ass to sleep." His eyes disappeared, and his footsteps echoes away.

How much longer I still had to spend in here was going to be the longest time of my life.

CHAPTER 17

JO

My heart pounded as I rolled up to the gate. *What the fuck am I doing here?* played on repeat in my head.

I hesitated as I entered to sign my paperwork as usual but as a visitor not as an employee. I should have been a thousand miles away from this city by now, but after my encounter with Laius's friend, Fort, as I'd learned to call him, I needed answers to the million questions what he told me carved in my brain.

Going through with the security check I should have been accustomed to by now, I still hated that pat-down as much as every time. Being touched for any reason was an intimate thing. Intimacy and I were strangers. I had no father, my mom's arms were ripped off me when I was eight, I'd been confined in a boarding academy for ten years after, and I'd only been intimate with one man in my whole life.

I was led down a long hallway that I hadn't passed through before to a dull, packed with loved ones of inmates waiting area. Anxiety wrapped around me as I waited to be called. It seemed like a thousand hours, and I contemplated leaving a thousand times. I brought a book out of my bag and began to read to take down the anxiety, but even my favorite hobby failed to take the edge off. I grabbed a pen and a sheet of paper and started writing. A list of the questions I had for Laius so I wouldn't forget any. Then I wrote down a reminder to burn this note as soon as possible. After the things Fort had told me, danger was much closer than I thought it'd be.

The guards called out a long list of names. Laius Lazzarini wasn't one of them. I started to worry this was going to be a blank visit. Did he refuse to see me? Or was he still in solitary confinement? Fort had told me I'd caused such cruel punishment. But he'd also told me, Laius's charges would be amended to self-defense and he'd be out soon. That meant the solitary punishment would be overruled.

"Laius Lazzarini!" the guard yelled the last name on the list. I spoke too soon.

My stomach tightened when they pulled open the door to the visitor's area. Out of instinct, I scanned the room to choose the most secluded table with the least surveillance exposure. There were two, but the best of them was taken by a beautiful woman my age in a sexy dress accentuating her massive breasts. I took the next best table and pressed my sunglasses up my nose.

My leg rocked under the table as I waited for the inmates' arrival, the room full with the low chatters and children's play sounds. Then the doors buzzed, and blue denim and chambray shirts streamed in.

There was no missing Furore even from across the room. He'd stand out with how beautiful he was whether it was a prison or a frat party. I was concerned about his safety as a very attractive man in a harsh place such as prison. Even with a body built to ruin and maim, and I knew he was feared and fully capable of taking care of himself, I needed him out of here. I needed him safe.

When his eyes locked right on me, I froze. He drew closer, my heart a wild rhythm with every step. I brought myself to rise and braced against the table. When he was in front of me, a man in front of a woman, not a student before his teacher, everything was different. My body primed with an attraction that no force or will could stop. My breath caught as I stood in his space, feeling the dominance he exuded wrapping around me, breaking my walls brick by brick, stripping me bare of the barricades I'd long set around me.

We stood rock solid for a long moment before he wrapped his arms around my waist and held me against his body. I gasped, but it came out muffled against his firm chest, and his scent filled my breath. Then I closed my eyes for a moment, a sudden peace falling over me when I was wrapped tight between his arms.

Something brushed the top of my head, and a sharp inhale followed as he pressed what must have been his nose to my hair. Then something hard dug into my stomach.

He didn't try to conceal it or pull away, as if he wanted me to feel him. Heat rushed between my thighs as desire unlike anything I'd ever known took hold of my body. "Laius," I whispered.

"When you say my name like that…" He broke our hug almost violently.

Instantly, I missed his warmth, feeling a painful, abrupt loss. I looked up at him, tongue tied. He didn't say anything either, but the way he was looking at me revealed more than words could. I ducked my head as I took a seat at the table, trying to pretend I didn't feel anything, not his hardness for me, not my wetness soaking my panties for him, not the inexplicable, shameful need to crawl back into his embrace and stay.

He didn't sit across from me. He took the seat to my left. It was probably so that people couldn't hear us, like I'd chosen the table away from the cameras. Or maybe it was because he wanted to…be closer to me.

Get these silly thoughts out of your head and do what you came here to do. "Thank you for seeing me," I murmured, mouth dry, unable to meet his eyes. I stared at the ink that covered his neck and chest. My fingers itched to reach out and touch the designs, so I folded them together in my lap.

"There will never be a time when I won't want to see you, *Miss Meneceo*."

I swallowed. "I'm glad you're out of solitary. I hate that I caused it."

"It's not your fault."

"You defended me."

"Something I'll be happy to do over and over."

Reflexively, I lifted my head to meet his gaze, those dark pools of green penetrating every part of me until they hit my soul. "I…I met your friend. He told me you sent him."

"I did. I trust Fort with my life. He's the best man to look after you while I'm here."

"Look after me? Is that what you call it? Did you know he jumped me at my building? He scared me to death."

Fury marred his face. "He did what?"

I didn't want him to get angry. He, for some unknown reason, was trying to look out for me, defending me and sending his friend to alert me. The last thing I wanted to do was causing Furore more trouble or be the cause of anything violent. "He said this wasn't his town. It belonged to *someone else*. He didn't know the best locations where no one would be watching. He didn't want to risk being seeing together so he used that *trick* to get me to meet him without being spotted."

"Did he fucking hurt you?" he asked with the same fury as if he didn't hear me.

"No, Laius. I mean, he's built like a wall and fighting him until he pushed me into my apartment has caused some inevitable bruises, but those are self-inflicted. He didn't hurt me. I wished there had been a more peaceful way to get me to meet him, but with how stubborn I was, it was probably the only way."

His gaze turned pensive, and his face calmed. Then he smirked. "You fought Fort?"

I chuckled. "I tried."

"You're a badass, *Miss Meneceo*."

I bit my lip, proud to hear it from him, and too aroused at the way he said my name. "Um...is it safe to talk here?"

He nodded once. "You chose a good table. Not the best, but it'll work."

"I have so many questions."

He leaned forward, his lips parting to speak, but then he paused and looked at my mouth. "You're so beautiful. Do you know how many times I pictured kissing you or how many times I said fuck it and almost did it right there in the middle of your class?"

I took a longer pause while my heart tried to beat out of my chest. My lips shivered, and I averted my gaze in a futile attempt to get a grip. "How long has your friend been following me?"

"A couple of weeks. I sent him to keep an eye on you for protection but without being noticed."

"So when he was at Belle View, he was watching over me? But he didn't say anything so no one would know who he was?"

"Brava."

I couldn't tell if it was genuine praise or he was making fun of me. "How do I know your friend isn't lying about the things he told me?"

He touched my chin with his finger, inducing another shiver as he directed my face back on his. "Ask me anything."

"Fort told me about the *family* that's looking for a lost Irish girl," I whispered. "They thought I was her, and they asked you to find out if it was true."

He nodded.

"So you've been lying all this time about everything—"

"Everything I've ever told you is the truth. I was never gonna give you to them. I'm not like that, Jo. I might be a monster but not that kind. From the second they showed me that photo of the little girl, I wanted to protect her. All I was doing was buying myself some time to show them I was game for my boy's sake."

"But you were trying to figure out who I was."

"Because I was convinced you were that girl. I wanted to know for sure so I'd make all the right moves to keep them away from you."

"And the time you tried to make me take off my sunglasses? What if I was her? How was that protecting me?"

"No one was looking. They were all focused on their homework, and you were standing too close to me, bending over, my body was shielding you from their eyes."

"But why?"

His tongue darted out of his mouth and licked his lower lip. "I'll tell you the same reason I told you then. I was tired of imagining the eyes I looked into when I fucked my fist every night. I wanted to know what they looked like for real."

My cheeks burned, and a wave of scorching heat descended down my neck and engulfed my breasts, which heaved in his face, and he stared.

"My eyes are up here," I said, but it didn't come out as either a warning or a complaint.

"But you're still hiding them from me. Until you quench my thirst for them, I'll feed my imagination with something else."

"You're so inappropriate."

"And you're not in a classroom anymore, *Miss Meneceo*. You're a single woman, visiting an inmate in prison, who is single, too. What do you think the *nature* of such visits is, baby girl?"

My jaw hung low. "I'm not here for…that." I protested even though *baby girl* caused not one but two throbs between my legs.

"Why are you here, Jo?"

Yes. Why was I here getting burned in a new hell I should do nothing but escape? Had I not had enough flames devouring me whole and spitting me flayed? Why could I not leave without seeing Laius Lazzarini one last time when I knew it'd only make me want to stay? Why was I here melting at words that would forever stir my wet dreams? Why was I here wanting, needing, them to be more than dreams? I cleared my throat. "I… I'm here to thank you for protecting me."

He chuckled. "I don't like to be lied to, especially when I've been nothing but honest with you."

"I'm not lying." I was only telling half the truth.

"Well, bless your heart, Jo. I stuck my neck out for you when you ain't even that girl. I'd been fucking myself in the dark, talking to myself like a crazy man because of it. If you're really here to thank me, a few words ain't gonna cut it, baby. You gotta show me how thankful you really are," he drawled like a Texan.

God, that accent turned my brain into mush. "What... How would you like me to thank you?"

"You see that table over there?" He didn't point. He just tilted his chin toward the secluded table I wanted to sit at but was taken. I nodded once.

"Do you know what people do when they sit there?"

I blinked toward the table. I could barely see the woman who sat there, and the inmate she was visiting didn't appear at all from here. Sweet Jesus. Now, I knew why she was wearing that sexy dress. Why did I have to be so naïve all the time? I had no clue people would... Not here. Not with all these people around. Not with the risk of being caught...or watched. I blushed hard. There was no question as to what Furore wanted.

He rose to his feet and subtly adjusted himself. Fuck, the glimpse of the outline alone was huge. "When I tell you to come, come." Then he winked. "Pun intended."

"No, Laius. I will not—"

He ignored me and was now talking to the people at the table. In a second, the other inmate was on his feet, protesting yet complying with Furore's wishes. Furore nodded for me to join him. Despite the other frowning man and glaring woman coming my way, who looked like they were about to murder me, I didn't have the courage to leave my seat because I knew deep down if I went there, I wouldn't have the willpower to deny Laius. Honestly, I was starting to think I'd give that man anything he asked for, and that was what terrified me the most.

CHAPTER 18

FURORE

"I will not have sex with you," she said under her breath, my favorite shade of red scorching her face as she threw a quick glance around the room. But no one was watching. We were in the corner away from the view of the guards and the cameras. I'd kept her safe from everyone else, but there was no one to keep her safe from me.

"Hey, look at me. Don't look at anyone else." I leaned closer, getting high on her scent. "Did you really think my first time inside you would be a quickie in a stinky place like this dump?"

"Then why did you bring me here?"

"Because you're driving me out of my fucking mind in that skirt," I said, and she fidgeted in her seat. My eyes roamed toward the buttons of her green shirt I was dying to undo so I could fill my grip with those tits, and then dropped down to her snug black skirt, to her ass that filled the chair and then some. "Fuck, you have the sexiest ass I've ever seen." I stared at her legs, wishing I could hike the fabric of her skirt up her thighs and then…

Blushing deep, she tucked her hair behind her ear, which I was still positive it was a wig. "Do you really have a son?"

I snorted with an eye roll. "You shittin' me right now?"

"Answer the question, please."

I pinched the bridge of my nose because she was trying to change the subject and the time we had left wasn't enough for half of the things I wanted to do to her. "Fine." I wanted her to believe and trust me. I wanted her to tell me the truth about her. She might not be the Larvin's kid, but she was someone else other than who she claimed to be. I wanted a lot from Jo Meneceo or whatever the fuck her real name was.

So, to save us both the time and the doubt, I told her everything about my boy and the bitch Delilah and her fucking husband. How I used the same scare tactic the Lanzas used on me and got Delilah to change her testimony. I'd sent Fort to Delilah offering her a choice. I wasn't gonna play the Lanzas' game, so McNamara was going to die. In that case, I'd rather I killed him myself. The choice was simple. She could either stick to her testimony and had her precious fucker in a grave or change her testimony and keep the asshole alive.

She knew I wasn't bluffing. If I was going down, it'd be with a bang. She also knew no one could protect her husband from the Mob but someone like the Night Skulls. We both put our past, pride and vendettas aside for now. She changed her testimony, and I assigned men to keep McNamara alive. It stung that I had to protect that piece of shit myself, but I'd do anything for a chance to be with my boy and my brothers. For a chance to be with the most beautiful girl I'd ever seen.

"Now, where were we?" With one hand I held her wrist under the table, and with the other I unfastened the front of my jeans. Her breath caught as I pulled my cock out and brought her hand to it.

"Laius, what are you—"

"No more questions, baby girl. Time to thank me." I closed her shaking fingers around me. Her jaw dropped as her fist explored the length and girth. She couldn't see me under the table, but she gasped when she finally found the end of my dick. I couldn't help the quiet groan that escaped me as I felt her hand on my cock for the first time, and I fucking pulsed in her fist. I widened my knees. "Stroke it up and down. It won't take long."

"What if we get caught?"

I smiled at how innocent she was, afraid of getting busted doing something wrong. "We won't. Just keep your eyes at me. Better if you take those goddamn shades off. I've already seen your eyes, why hide them from me?"

Her fist started moving, and the way she licked her lip when she did almost made me nut on the spot. "Do you like hazel eyes?"

"I like *you*, Jo. Even if you were fucking blind."

She swallowed, and the sound of her breathing became higher. Her fingers trembled around me and almost slipped.

"Hey, eyes on me. Only on me," I commanded, keeping her hand steady on my erection. The way she was nervous, while so fucking sexy, could draw unwanted eyes on us.

"Why do you like me?"

No clue. I'd imagined her lush curves naked in my bed, fantasized about every way I could put my dick in her, and then dreamed about holding her at night. I imagined her on the back of my bike and wearing my cut. I didn't know what it was or why, but she had me consumed, maybe even obsessed. I'd never experienced something like this. The need for one certain woman and no one else. "I said enough questions. It's my turn to ask. Have you touched yourself thinking of me, baby girl?"

She gasped, and then she gasped again when she spread my pre-cum around the crown and her finger found the little holes in my cock. The piercings for the jewelry they took when I got in. "What is this?"

"I'll tell you when you grow up."

"I'm serious. Are you hurt?"

The way she was genuinely concerned about me made my heart roar. "Are you worried about me or my cock? Don't worry, baby, I can fuck you into next week. No problem there."

"Laius, please, who did this to you?"

I laughed. "No one, baby. It's a cock piercing but without the metal because those fuckers won't allow them here. Never seen one before?"

She just shook her head in awe.

"There's so much I'll show you for the first time, baby girl. Now answer my question and don't you dare lie to me."

Her head dropped, as if in shame, as she nodded. Fuck. She couldn't just do that and not be specific. I wanted all the details. Her innocence was fucking killing me. I needed to ruin this girl bad. But first I'd toy with her, see if that blush could go any deeper. "You're so bad, touching yourself to your own student, Miss Meneceo. You naughty little girl."

"Please…I'm ashamed enough."

She really was ashamed. *Girl, you don't know what shame is.* There was nothing wrong with her wanting me. Not to me. I fucking wanted her, too. *That* was fucking wrong, but I didn't give a shit. "Spread your legs and pull your skirt up."

Her head jerked up. "What?"

"Do as I say."

She took a moment, but this time she didn't look around and opened her knees and pulled the end of the skirt to the top of her thighs.

"More."

Her hand faltered on my cock before she obeyed and showed me her panties. Fuck. They were pink just like that skirt she wore at the last class, and it was quickly becoming my favorite color.

I hissed as I took in the wet spot growing on them, and her hand dipped low and squeezed more pre-cum from me. "Fuck. Pull them to the side. I wanna see your pretty pussy."

She did as I said. The wetness trickling on her inner thighs showed she loved me telling her what to do. "Fuck, baby, I wanna taste you." My fingers reached for her. She trembled and gave a little moan at my touch as I coated two fingers with her wetness and then I sucked them. My eyes rolled in bliss. "Scratch that. I don't want just a taste. I wanna fucking devour you until you come all over my mouth and then lick it all off."

Her breath stuttered on her lips, and her hand stroked me harder. I gazed at her, flushed and naughty as she rubbed me while her pussy was naked in public. Fuck. I could come just like that. "Easy on the hand, baby. Let me take care of you first."

"H-here?"

"Yes. Just keep looking at me and try to be quiet…although there's nothing more I'd love to hear but your moans when I turn them to screams."

Her lips twitched with a shy smile. That was probably the first time I saw her smile, and I was fucking floored. That girl was gonna own my fucking soul.

With her fingers, she spread herself for me. When I saw the pink inside, the animal in me salivated. That pussy was mine. I needed to fuck her, be inside her, claim the fuck out of her.

I dipped one finger in while I circled her clit. She was fucking drenched, and I envied every motherfucker that got to coat his dick with her honey. I couldn't wait to get out of here so I'd feel her clench and throb around me.

"Why are you really here, Jo?" I rubbed her faster, watching her soaking my hand.

"I…I told you."

"Why are you *really* here?"

Her breasts fell and rose with her labored breath. "I…I just…"

"I won't let you say goodbye to me." It wasn't hard to see it. She was here to get closure and leave everything behind. "You can't leave, Jo. You can't leave me. Wait for me, baby. I know you think I'm dangerous and staying anywhere near me after what you've learned could get you in trouble, but I'll be out in no time, and you'll be safe until I'm there, I promise. Then I'll take over, and no one will ever dare come near you. Just sit tight and wait for me, baby, all right?"

"Laius…" she whispered, her hips moving forward, wanting more of me. Then she started stroking me again. "I'm so close. I want you to come with me."

My teeth speared my lip at how fucking hot that was. "I'd fucking love to, baby girl. But promise me first. Please."

"How about I take off my sunglasses, and you look me in the eyes when you come, like you've always wanted…then we'll see if you still want me to make that promise?"

My brows hooked in confusion, but I was too caught in the sounds her pussy made and the way her fist on my cock felt to care. "Okay, baby. Okay."

Her fingertips quivered on the edge of the shades. Then she swallowed and took them off. Her eyes were closed until she took a deep breath, killing me with anticipation as I waited for the moment I'd finally come with our eyes locked on each other.

Then she opened them and gazed at me.

"Fuck...me." All my blood rushed down to my dick. My balls tightened, and I bit down on a groan. I pointed my cock straight at her pussy and came. Marking her. Claiming her mine. She creamed hard. Fuck, the face she made and the little sounds she couldn't contain... The beauty of her eyes and the danger behind them matched those of the thick ropes of my cum splattered all over her naked, wet pussy and the insides of her thighs, leaking into her own cum.

Jo was heaven. The only heaven I'd go to.

Her hand left my cock as she let go of her panties, covering my cum, keeping it on her, with her. If that wasn't the sexiest thing I'd ever seen...

I tucked my cock back in my jeans as she closed her legs and pulled her skirt down. The clock chimed, announcing the end of our time together. I saw the disappointment in her eyes that mirrored mine, but also I saw the concern. When she reached for her shades, I stopped her hand in its tracks. "I need to see you again."

"Even after you knew the truth?"

"Especially after I knew the truth. Promise me, Jo. Promise me you'll come back tomorrow. I don't think I can wait until I'm out. I promise you, you'll be safe. I won't let anything hurt you. But, please, come back tomorrow."

She lifted the most eccentric pale greenish blue eyes at me. The ones that enchanted me from the first moment I saw them. Then she blinked in disbelief before she hid her gaze from me with those fucking shades. "I think—"

I grabbed her into my embrace and held her tight, never wanting to let go. "You will not leave me, Jo. Never," I whispered in her ear. "You're mine now. My cum in your panties proves it. You're mine, and you know it. I'm not asking, baby girl. You *will* come back tomorrow, Jocasta Larvin."

CHAPTER 19

JO

Jo Meneceo. Formerly Fiona Andrews. Originally Jocasta Larvin or should have been if my father had bestowed me with his royal name. He never did, so I took my mother's last name. Jocasta Kelly.

I should have been a daughter to a king. A princess. Instead, I'd lived as a pauper, an unwanted bastard, a liability at risk of losing her life at any time. And now, at twenty-three, I was officially a slut. I literally was driving home with a man's cum on my pussy. A man, my own student, came on me, in a prison.

I'd never felt dirtier in my whole life, yet it didn't bother me. In fact, I had this silly grin on my face all the way back to my apartment, and I'd thought I'd never smile again. Not after all the trauma and sadness I'd known nothing but in my life. And not after Tirone. Not so quickly, anyway. All it took was having an orgasm by the hand of a gangster biker as he shot his cum on my pussy in a wild place like prison while fifty people surrounded us, some of them holding weapons.

Yup, a total slut.

Staring at the boxes cluttering my bedroom, I found myself going back and forth about finishing packing them. Part of me still thought starting over somewhere else was the right and the safest thing to do. Another part, the one possessed by a mind haunting orgasm, was dying to go back to San Quentin—to Furore—tomorrow, without an ounce of fear or worry of what might be the consequences.

My hand traveled to my panties, reminding me of the epic debauchery I'd just indulged in, like I'd ever forget. No matter what, I'd always remember the day I pulled my skirt up for a prisoner, pulled my panties to the side, let him come on me while he rubbed the shit out of my clit until I came for him, too. I stared down at my soiled underwear, the evidence this wasn't a dream or a scene from a book I loved so much I pretended I lived it for real.

I should take them off, though. I should shower and take the prison smell off me. My nose skimmed the fabric of my shirt where Furore's scent lingered. I expected he'd be filthy, but he didn't smell bad at all. Yes, there were hints of cigarettes and sweat, but the majority of it was him, his so manly scent that had set my vagina fluttering then and now at the reminder.

I circled my clit on top of my panties, my eyes hooded at the feeling. What would happen if I touched myself while his cum was still on me?

You're so dirty. Just go shower and finish packing so you can put all this behind you and go.

While I agreed with the sane part of my inner voice, I found myself stretching on the bed, sprawled with my hand sliding into my center. "Just one more time, then I'll go."

I unbuttoned my shirt and pulled my breast out of the bra. Then I flicked my nipple and squeezed. Something I'd have loved if he'd done. I rubbed at my clit, picturing the plum sized crown of his massive cock doing the work. I wished I'd had the courage and peeked under the table to see him so I could have the full picture now.

My lip curled under my teeth as I imagined his cock with the jewelry on. I'd looked up cock piercings on my way home. The website listed a set of benefits to the jewelry for the sexual partner that I'd love to experience. And I had to admit they looked hot and whoever had them must have been a fearless badass. It seemed I had a thing for dangerous, badass men who rode bikes, were over the top jealous and possessive and didn't care enough for the law.

Don't you dare think about Tirone. Ever. Just Furore. Just this one time and then never again.

Closing my eyes, listening to Laius's voice talking dirty in those husky whispers, I touched myself. Seeing only the dark arousal in his gaze behind my eyelids, I moaned. My fingers lifted to my nose for a second so I could smell his seed, the little souvenir he'd left for me and marked me with, and the pressure gathering down my belly intensified.

God, I shouldn't desire Laius Lazzarini as much as I did, but he was taking over me without permission. He was so hot, in command, powerful, and above all he was protecting me even though he didn't have to. He liked me for me, and he wasn't afraid of who I was. After all he'd learned about me, he liked me. He wanted me. He demanded I stayed.

I don't want just a taste. I wanna fucking devour you until you come all over my mouth and then lick it all off.

I clenched hard, rubbing frantically, chasing the orgasm—

Ring!

My eyes snapped open. *Ring! Ring!*

Swearing at the timing, I darted a glare at the drawer when I hid the burner, but that wasn't where the ringing coming from. That was the goddamn landline. Who would call me on it? Nobody ever did, not even the school.

I straightened up and fixed my clothes, panting, swearing again. I was this close to coming. Whoever was calling was going to get a piece of my mind. As I clawed at the handset, a sudden fright invaded me. What if it was Ty?

My heart thrashed as I tried to control my breathing. My eyes squeezed as I picked up the phone. "H-hello?"

"Hello. This is a collect call from Laius Lazzarini, an inmate at San Quentin State Prison. This service is provided by Tel Communications. For rate information, press one now. To accept this call, press three now. To block all future calls, press—"

I pressed three fast, relieved and a bit stunned.

"Call accepted. Thank you for using Tel Communications. This call will be recorded and is subject to monitoring at any time. You may begin speaking."

"Buonasera, *Miss Meneceo*," Laius said, and despite the frustration I was interrupted at the worst of times and the slight moment of panic this call had caused me, a huge grin hurt my cheeks along with the heat the burst in them.

"Good evening to you, too, *Furore*." I tried to make it sexy, throwing in a pathetic Italian accent, as he always did with my name, but it sounded like an embarrassment.

"Your Italian is getting better." He chuckled. "I prefer Laius from you, though, baby. Say it for me."

"Laius," I whispered, butterflies in my stomach as if I were a shy school girl getting her first call from the quarterback who had just said he liked her. Except the quarterback was an outlaw biker, twice my age, and I was his teacher.

He groaned. "Fuck… You know I haven't washed my hand yet? I keep sniffing at it like a crackhead. Did you shower?"

I cleared my throat, my whole body burning with shame and arousal at what he'd said and what I'd been doing right before he called. "Um…this call is monitored. How did you get this number?"

"I have my ways. Don't be shy on me now. Tell me."

I shook my head as if he could see me. "I…I was about to. And before you ask, no, I'm not going to take the phone with me or describe anything for you when I'm in the shower."

He laughed. "Why didn't you do it right away?"

"How do you know I haven't just arrived home?"

"Baby," he said as if saying, *"C'mon, are you kidding me?"*

It felt good that he was keeping an eye on me. Since Tirone left, I hadn't felt really safe. Not until I met Fort the other day and knew the Night Skulls were watching over me. Not until I knew the smell of Laius Lazzarini's hug and the feeling of his protective arms.

"Okay. Well, I was…um…reminiscing…but your call stopped me at a crucial timing, and now some parts of me, two to be exact, are blue."

There was a pause. "Fuck. You're driving me crazy, baby girl. I hate that you need me, and I can't be there yet."

You're here now. I didn't say it. There was no way in hell I was going to have phone sex over a prison collect call.

"I'll make it up to you tomorrow, I promise," he said.

"What makes you so sure I'll be there tomorrow?" I teased.

"Because I said so, and you're my good girl."

My nipples hardened and a fresh gush of arousal melted my panties. "No, I'm a very naughty girl. I think we've established that today."

"Oh yeah? I gotta punish you then."

"Is that so? How?"

"No more *reminiscing* until tomorrow. Until I show you the rest of my punishment."

Fuck. I could come just at the anticipation of what he planned for me the next time I saw him. "Laius…I don't know…"

"You can't be that cruel, baby, and let me miss you like that." His voice dropped, the playfulness gone.

I sighed. I was going to miss him, too. I was missing him already. How could that be happening? We'd only known each other for a few weeks, when we practically fought every time we met, when I thought he was an enemy about to destroy my life. How could everything change in one day?

"Jo? Still there?"

"Yes."

"Do you remember what I said today before you left?"

You're mine now. My cum in your panties proves it. You're mine, and you know it. "Every word."

"Good. Because I don't like to repeat myself."

"What's that supposed to mean?"

"It means you can't run from me. I won't let you. So you'd better be there tomorrow, baby girl."

The threatening tone of his, while toxic, wreaked havoc on my body. I blamed Tirone for it. He was the only boyfriend I'd ever had. My first love and the boy who took my virginity. My body responded to his toxicity no matter how much my brain resisted it. He was always threatening me because of his jealousy and over the top possessiveness. Furore was exhibiting the same tendencies, and while I should be running as far away from it as possible, I was drawn to it like moth to a flame. "Or else?"

"If the mark I left on you isn't enough to make you understand you're mine, I'll have to claim you some other way, baby. I can't promise I'll be gentle the next time, though."

"What's that supposed to mean?"

"Come tomorrow, and you'll never have to know. Wear something pink."

CHAPTER 20

JO

My body loved the threat. My brain screamed at me to run for the hills. There was a thrill to the forbidden and a kick in breaking the rules. To be the object of desire to someone who didn't take no for an answer that he'd destroy anything in the way to have you, even you. To want what you couldn't have, to crave what destroyed you.

I had that with Ty. Why would I want it again with Laius?

It had to stop. No matter how much I wanted him, I couldn't repeat the same mistake and expect a different result. Furore and I would end the same way Ty and I did. In pain, tears and heartbreak. The only way.

I refused to remain in that narrative when I was treated as property only to be disowned later. A disgrace. Something to be used for twisted men's pleasure and then tossed away when they were done. I'd learned my lesson, which I should have learned way earlier, even before Ty, because I saw what happened to the women who did that. I refused to become like my mother. I wasn't Madeline Kelly, and I wouldn't meet the same destiny.

I didn't care if the thought of Laius alone made me smile or that his touch was the only source of happiness there was in my life when I was certain I was going to be alone forever, trapped in a bleak life enforced by the danger that would always surround me.

I didn't care if he said he was going to protect me because even if he'd proven he was capable, even if I believed he meant it now, once he was done with me—and he would because that was what my father did to Mom and what Tirone did to me despite their promises—I'd be in danger again and piling up more heartaches.

You couldn't overlook all the red flags and expect something good to come out of it, right? Declan Larvin was a mafia boss, a criminal who broke the law and took lives on a daily basis, not to mention he was a cheater. How could Mom have expected he would have protected her or me?

And I, an idiot who repeated her mistake falling for another toxic man, *boy*, who at seventeen wasn't afraid of breaking the law— and I didn't just mean sleeping with his teacher—who constantly used me for his pleasure, whispering false and dark promises in my ears, manipulating me emotionally to keep me while he'd been planning a disappearing act all along. How could I have expected him to live up to such promises of love, protection and forever?

Furore, although different from those two men because he'd demonstrated several acts of both honesty and chivalry, wasn't any less toxic. He was an outlaw and one of those who took what they wanted whenever they wanted. How could I expect his promises to last as long as *I*, not *he*, wanted them to last?

We had our fun, Furore and I, but that was it. That was why I was here at the gates, filling another form to visit him. He had to know, face to face, it was over.

As I walked down the hallway after the security check, I practiced my speech. I

needed to be firm so he'd know I was
determined to—

A hand grabbed me and pulled me toward
a side door swinging open. My heart stopped,
and so did my brain for a second. Then I
recognized the tattoos on the arm.

The door closed behind us as he pulled me
into the pitch black room. "Furore, what the
hell?"

"Is *what the hell* very creative, Miss
Meneceo? I know you can do better than
that." His lips crashed down on my mouth
and claimed mine.

Giddy, too lost in the swirl of emotions
showering me in that kiss, our first kiss, I
forgot everything I'd practiced to say to him. I
forgot the reason I came here and all the
lectures I'd been giving myself all the way. All
fear and danger and logic abandoned me. All
that was left was hunger and need that could
only be fulfilled by Laius's lips.

His hand held me by the back of my neck,
as if I were a cat he was petting, but he didn't
tangle his fingers in my hair as he pulled me
tight against his hard body. Did he know that
wasn't my hair?

I couldn't wonder or ask because my whole
attention was consumed by the tongue
slipping past my lips, taking without

permission. My mouth parted wider in surrender. The part of me I'd been fighting all night and all day, the part that wanted him to have every inch of me he desired, to be used for his pleasure, to submit to his dominance no matter how toxic, triumphed over everything else.

In that kiss, I fell backwards. In his lips I drowned back into my old ways, and I didn't give a shit.

DIRTY SLUT.

"I wanna see you," he groaned, his hand leaving my neck. Light flooded the room as he flipped a switch, and I was grateful for my sunglasses.

I took in the place and realized we were in some sort of a holding cell. Then my heart dipped when I discovered we weren't alone. There was a guard in the room.

"Don't pay attention to him. He's good," Laius said.

"Good? What do you mean *good?*"

"It means for the next fifteen minutes, he's guarding *us.*"

"In exchange for what? Watching?" I was sick to my stomach.

The guard cleared his throat and gave us his back. Then he pretended to be busy with his phone.

"No, baby. You see that new, shiny phone he's playing with? That's his reward. I'm not ready to share you." Laius brushed his calloused fingers over my cheek. "I don't think I'll ever be ready to share you."

"You share a lot of women?"

He slid the sunglasses off my face and made sure I was hidden entirely from the guard's view. "Every time I look into your eyes, something tells me I won't share another woman ever again."

My lashes fluttered, and so did my heart. I couldn't help the little moan that fled my chest. His lips glided under my earlobe and across my jaw and chin. Grinding his erection into my stomach, he seared my skin with his tongue. Then his hand found my neck again, this time closing on my throat.

His eyes roamed hungrily over my body. "Did you do as you were told?"

Breath stuck in my throat, I managed to cock a brow at him.

He stared at my outfit again. A sky blue shirt and an orange summer skirt. Nothing pink. He slid his hand under my skirt and cupped my pussy. I gasped as he gave it a little squeeze before he lifted my skirt to see the color of my panties. Orange like the skirt.

He glared at me, squeezing tighter on my neck and pussy. "You really want to be punished, naughty girl, don't ya?"

I drenched his palm with my wetness, but I kept my defiant look. His hand on my pussy traveled to my butt and smacked. I hissed, but I didn't fold. He pinched me, and God if I didn't enjoy it, the punishment while *I* was doing the teasing for once.

He unbuttoned my shirt, his fingers on my chest leaving a trail of flames, ripping another hiss from me. "You love to drive me nuts, don't you, baby?"

Guilty, I smirked. Then when he pushed open my shirt, I knew I won this round.

"Fuck, baby." He stared at my breasts, at the pink bra I was hiding underneath. "Why didn't you just say you were my good girl all this time?"

"Who said I want to be your good girl?" I did, but I wanted to tease him more. I wanted *him* to make me his good girl. I needed to earn it.

He licked his lip before his mouth swooped down on the visible parts of my breasts, licking, biting, devouring. "Fine. Be a bad girl. As long as you're mine." Then he pulled them out, took them in with a feral gaze and feasted on my nipples. "You're so fucking hot." He groaned, and it sounded painful, the need he had for me intoxicating.

His gaze held me captive. It was always the fucking eyes. The way he looked at me, the way he couldn't keep his hands off me as if he couldn't survive another day without having me, dulled away all caution and sense. Under his gaze and touch, I was a bundle of twisted need that craved his attention and nothing else.

He bent a little, and both his big hands were on my boobs, pushing them together. He groaned again as he stared at them. "I wanna cram my cock between your tits and then come all over them."

My thighs rubbed together with the tangling, sweet pain between them. I loved the way he dirty talked to me. It brought me to a different level of arousal. My fingers tangled in his hair as he sucked hard on my nipple, and I realized this was the first time I touched him without any guidance from him. His hair was so soft yet thick enough to bury my fingers in. I pulled him closer as he tugged and pinched my other nipple, loving the pain of his roughness and the hunger he was showing for my flesh.

"Yes, touch me, baby." He noticed. "I'm yours like you're mine."

I started to unbutton his shirt, doing a lousy job because I couldn't concentrate on a task as simple as working a few buttons. It took a substantial time, but I finally reached the last button and realized just now he wasn't wearing anything under it. He shrugged off the shirt for me, and…*the woman was too stunned to speak.*

He was muscular, but I didn't think he was that ripped. He'd looked rather on the lean side with his clothes on, but those shoulders, that chest, those abs and that fucking Adonis belt… He was rippling with sinewy muscles and angry tattoos. The perfect amount of muscle and flesh and dark art.

Then I touched him. I dared let my fingers feel the toned sculpture of his body. "Oh God."

"That's right, baby. I'm your god. Now, I need you to be a good girl for me and show me what's mine."

In a trance, I just pulled my skirt up. His hands were fast on the panties, ripping them out, and then he lifted them to his nose. He grunted and hissed, his eyes pinned on mine, growing darker, almost black with arousal. His breath grew louder as he shoved them in his pocket. "I'm keeping these until the next time I see you." The sound of his zipper coming undone tore into the silence, and my heart skipped a beat.

"I wanted to wait for this, but I just can't. I have to have you now." He wrapped my legs around his waist, his erection poking my hip. "Hold tight."

Dazed, I couldn't believe I was in a cell, spreading my legs for a prisoner, about to be fucked by the most gorgeous gangster biker, where an officer kept watch.

My eyes darted at the guard. The back of his bowed head stared at me, yet it triggered something in me. Sanity.

"Don't look away from me, Jo," Furore commanded. "Keep your eyes on me."

"No."

"No?"

I shook my head, a sudden wakeup call ringing in my head. "Put me down. I'm done."

"Done with what, baby?"

"Being a dirty whore." That was what I was. With Tirone and now with Furore. "This needs to stop. I have to stop."

"You're not *a* dirty whore. You're *my* dirty whore." He bit my earlobe and gave me a playful kiss. "My princess, too. I promise once I'm outta here, I'll spoil the fuck out of you, baby."

"Until you're done with me."

"What?"

All my traumas and insecurities came down on me at once. "Until you don't want me anymore, and then you'll throw me away. Then I'll be *a* dirty whore that loathes herself for letting more people abuse her like that."

He scowled at me. Then he put me down carefully yet angrily. His palms caught either side of my face as his eyes bore into me. "Who did this to you before? What motherfucking loser had you and then dared leave you? Who fucking called you a dirty whore, Jo? I'll rip their fucking tongue out of their throat and shove it up their ass."

I blinked. Hard. I didn't expect that response. I didn't expect *anything* from him.

"Answer me, baby, who fucking did this? Who fucking hurt you? I'll kill them."

"No one," I answered fast. I didn't want him to hurt anyone on my behalf. Mostly, because I didn't want him to get hurt or go back to prison when he was about to be free. I was as protective of him as he was of me. I had to admit, though, it felt good to have someone defending you like that. Someone who cared enough to stand up for you. Someone who wasn't afraid to go the extra mile to protect you, to make you feel worthy of love.

"Jo, I'm your man now," he said as a warning. "You have to tell me so I can take care of you."

The fuzzy feelings he was inducing in me convoluted my thoughts. Instead of embracing them and allowing them in, worry and suspicion took over. "You don't even know me. You can't possibly... Why are you trying to—"

"Don't even say it."

He looked hurt, but that let suspicion crawl up higher in me. Why would a man like him be soft and gentle and caring to me? Why risk anything for a stranger like me? Why was he so eager to make me believe he genuinely liked me and was willing to do anything for me?

Someone like me that was marked by shame, guilt, abandonment and danger couldn't be desired that much. Wasn't worth that much. It couldn't be real. Right? He was manipulating me. But why? It couldn't be just to get in my pants. I wasn't that pretty either.

Could it be another bet? The first to bring the slut teacher in a cell and fuck her would win ten packs of cigarettes. My panties were proof, and the guard was the witness.

It didn't make any sense, though. He was going out. He wouldn't care about winning because he wasn't staying long enough. Then what the fuck was it?

"Listen, Furore, whatever your game is, I don't want to play."

"What fucking game? Everything I've told you and done for you so far isn't enough to prove I'm not playing?"

It should have been, but I wasn't wired to believe I deserved any love or happiness. If my own father didn't want me, if he'd allowed his wife to send men over to kill me, if the only man that said he loved me dumped me without so much of a word, then how was I supposed to believe anyone else when they said they cared? "I came here today to tell you that it's over."

He snorted as his stare dropped to my boobs that were still out and his cock that was digging a hole in my stomach. "Over? Baby, we haven't even started yet."

Blushing, I tucked my breasts in and fixed my skirt. "I'm sorry, but I need to leave." I was ruining everything, but sooner or later things would be ruined anyway. It was best if I did it now myself. "I wish you the best in life and hope you can reconnect with your son."

I didn't take two steps before he grabbed my wrist and pinned me to the wall. Then his mouth crushed mine in a demanding, violent kiss. He bit my lips so hard I thought I was bleeding, but he stopped right before, and then his fist cupped my jaw. "If I was using you, if I wanted to fucking hurt you, I'd have done it already and you couldn't have done anything about it. I put my neck out on the line for you, and you still think I'm speaking out of my ass? You still can't tell that I'm crazy about you, that I wanna make you mine?"

"Because it doesn't make any sense. You can't want me like that, not that much."

"Yeah?" He grabbed my thighs and hooked me around his hips. Then he guided the tip of his cock to my entrance. "How about now?"

I gasped and whimpered as I squirmed in his grip. Split in half, part of me wanted to bear down on him and make him take care of the pain I couldn't reach, the other part screamed at me to run. "Laius, please, let me go."

"No." He moved the crown of his cock in and out of me in shallow thrusts. "Not before I make you mine."

Fear thudded in my chest and shamefully made me wetter. "No. Please. I—"

"You don't have a say in it. Not anymore. You knew what would happen when you came yesterday, and when you came back today. You know I'm never letting you go. I warned you, Jo, but you didn't listen."

"No, no, you can't do this."

"I can and I will. You're mine."

"Not like that. Please, I'm begging you, let me leave."

"Oh, you'll be begging all right, but not for that." He thrust a little deeper, but not too deep. "You know why, baby? Because as much as I want to feast on your sweet cunt, give you an orgasm you'll never forget and then fuck you right after to show you a glimpse of what we're gonna have together, I won't." He rocked his hips, entering me but only teasing. Torturing me. "No pleasure for you, naughty girl. I'm giving you just the tip, leaving you wanting more so you'll come beg for it later. Then I'll decide if I wanna give it to you because I own your orgasms now, baby. And I'm fucking coming inside you now so you'll know who fucking owns you and your cunt."

With a groan and a few faster tormenting strokes that were meant to grow the painful need not to ease it, his face hardened as his cum poured thick and hot inside of me bare.

He devoured my lips as I clenched around the tip, rubbing myself in a desperate attempt to get any kind of relief.

He'd marked me for the second time, sealing his ownership of me.

If I hadn't believed him before, I believed him, at least, when he said I was going to beg for him and the kind of pleasure I now understood only he could give me. And I believed him when he said I didn't have a say in it anymore.

Everything was clear in my head, and every doubt I had about my decisions vanished. I belonged to Laius Lazzarini. I belonged to the president of the Night Skulls.

I belonged to Furore.

CHAPTER 21

FURORE

My cut. My bike. My freedom. Nothing could beat having all three of them again. Nothing but the two faces I'd yearned to see the first thing I was out of the gates and neither was there.

Fort's big arms choked and squeezed me. "Freedom, brother! I got a killer party down at Rosewood for you. The place is torched, but some parts of it were still salvageable. I reckoned it'd be a crack house by now, but lucky people were still afraid of the Night Skulls all this time and never even dared come close to the notorious compound." He barked a laugh. "I got some bitches hanging there for you, buddy. We're gonna eat pussy for dinner and get our cocks royally sucked."

I stared at the parking lot where there was no Jo or Rex. "Where's he? Where's Jo?"

"Bro, you know how your boy can be, but he'll come around. We all did. Look, I'll tell him to come to Rosewood tonight, and if he still doesn't show, I'll go bring him to the party myself. Trust me. When he sees the pussy, he'll want to stay." He laughed again, walking me to where our bikes stood.

"And Jo?"

"I don't know, man. She was at her place this morning."

"Then?"

"Then I had to bring your bike from Delilah's and park it here, and then get my ass back to you."

"Why didn't you bring her with you?"

He scratched his head. "Uh…aren't we supposed to be low key so we wouldn't grab unwanted attention to her? Or was I busting my ass, sneaking around to keep an eye on her without being tailed for no reason?"

"That was before. Now, I'm out. Every motherfucker out there needs to know she's mine." I straddled my bike. "Let's go."

"To Rosewood?"

"To Jo."

"What about the party? Ya think it's the best place to bring her to, bro?"

"Fort, I appreciate you doing all that shit for me and all, but I don't give a damn about any other pussy than what's already mine, all right?"

"You sure it's yours, Prez?"

I glared at him. "The fuck that means?"

"Look around ya. She ain't here. She knows you're getting out of the Arena today, and she's a no show. It says something."

"Fuck you, *bro*. Jo is mine, and she knows it. She's just young and likes to be chased, so what?"

He stared at me like I was a crazy stranger. "Who are you and what did you do to my friend? Since when do you chase, Furore?"

Since a pair of Irish eyes squeezed my dead heart alive.

CHAPTER 22

JO

Hidden in my car, using a burner, I dialed the number I promised myself once I left Chicago I'd never call again.

He picked up right away. "I've been waiting for your call," he said in his Italian accent and calm tone. "How are you doing, topolina?"

Tears sprung to my eyes the moment I heard his voice. "I'm…I'm well."

"No, you're not. You're crying. What happened? Are you safe?"

"Yes, yeah. Don't worry about me. Nothing happened."

"Yet. Nothing happened yet."

"What do you mean, Michele? Do you know something?"

"I need you to come home so I can take care of you. I've only kept my distance all these years because I respected your wishes, but now, you need to come back where I can protect you. You fooled the Lanzas for now, but it won't be for long."

"You knew? Of course, you did. You and they are close."

"A lot has changed since you left, Jo. Things will change even more and not for the better. There's a war coming, and I don't want you anywhere near it."

"That's why I left, Michele, and you know it." I didn't want anything to do with any mob. Even if Michele was the one who saved me that night, gave me a new identity and hid me in Bellomo Academy. I was grateful and forever indebted to him, but that wasn't a life I wanted for myself. Once I finished school and became eighteen, I had to get out and start a life on my own without any relation or interference from the mob for this exact reason, for not getting anywhere near a mafia war.

"That's not the way. There are things in life we don't choose but we cannot escape. Let me take care of you the way it should be done. The Night Skulls cannot be trusted, Jo."

He knew about Laius, too? "I trust *him*."

He sighed. "Oh, my sweet girl. You can't. There's so much you don't know. The Lanzas and the Night Skulls of San Francisco had always had business together."

"But Furore's chapter is in Texas, and he wants nothing to do with the Lanzas. You know how they are in the South."

"Enzio Lanza has good connections with the cartel in Mexico more than he leads on. He has a good chance to run the South if the Irish help him. If that happens, Lazzarini and his club won't be able to stop him. Have you ever considered that he might have turned the Lanzas' offer so he'd trade you himself?"

I shook my head in disbelief. "For what?"

"Keeping his turf. If *he* helps the Larvins, they won't help the Lanzas."

My jaw dropped. How had that possibility never crossed my mind? But no. It couldn't be. He wouldn't do this to me. Not after… "He…he did things." I didn't hide anything from Michele. He was the only father figure I'd ever had. But I was too embarrassed to tell him that Laius, when he didn't know I was on birth control, came inside me bare in a prison cell. A man didn't do that to a woman he was going to deliver to her demise. "He still protected me even when he thought I was someone else."

Another sigh. "You think his life is better than ours, topolina? You think he can protect you better than I can?"

"No. I owe you my life, Michele. Everything I am today wouldn't be if it weren't for you. And I know his life is as brutal and dangerous as the one I ran from, the one you're now telling me I can't escape. But if it's inevitable to lead such a life, can I, at least, get to choose how to spend it and with whom?"

"And you choose Laius Lazzarini of all people?"

"He makes me happy, papà," I cried.

He didn't speak right away. "You're hitting heavy with your words, topolina. I haven't heard you say it in years."

"I mean it when I say it. I wish you were my real father, Michele."

"I should have been." His voice got thick with emotion, and more tears streamed down my face. "Anyway, if he made you happy, why didn't you go see him yesterday?"

"Wow." I wiped my face, sniveling. "You really kept your distance, huh?"

"You know I'll always watch over you. Now, answer me. Why aren't you with him? I can't imagine you want my permission."

A troubled moan fled my chest. "I didn't go see him because I'm afraid." I didn't want to fail again, yet I knew I was bound to. "I'm afraid he won't want me after he finds out what I've done. I fucked up, papà. Big time."

"La mia topolina tutta speciale," he chuckled.

"You know I couldn't learn that language no matter how hard you tried to teach me. What are you saying?"

"You're a special girl, Jo. And kind and innocent. Whatever you think you've done, he's done worse. Way worse. What do you think he does for a living?"

My lips twisted. I didn't want to know the details. If his chapter was anything like the one that used to be here... "How illegal are we talking about? Narcotics? Guns?" I sighed. "Trafficking?"

"Not the trafficking."

A sliver of relief washed over me, yet it didn't make the club Laius ran any less illegal.

"Do *you* think you'll want him after you know what he's done and what he continues to do? And don't compare him to me. I'm your father. He's going to be your man. You'll share a life, and his sins will become yours."

"I think I love him enough to accept him and his sins."

"Love?"

I laughed and cried at the same time, at how ridiculous that must have sounded. It was too soon and too dangerous and too wrong. I meant, even our names were dooming us to a tragedy. Jocasta and Laius? Really? What was next? I had his son who would grow up to kill him and marry me? "It's… Yes. I think I'm in love with Furore."

He didn't respond for a long time I had to check the phone to see if the call was disconnected. "Michele?"

"Listen, Jo. I don't approve of your relationship with Lazzarini, but you don't need my approval or blessing. If you truly think you love him and he can make you happy, then you have to go and be with him. Just promise me you won't tell him how we're connected yet. Not until *I* can trust him with you. Do you hear me, topolina?"

"Yes," I said, starting the car.

"Then promise me."

I wasn't planning on hiding anything from Laius. I trusted him that much, but I couldn't say no to Michele either. "I promise," I said as

I checked the GPS and looked through the windshield to make sure for the millionth time that I was heading toward the right place. Rosewood. The Night Skulls' compound where Laius had told me he was staying in an angry message after he promised to *punish* me for not being there yesterday outside of the Arena or at my place when he'd come looking for me.

My vagina buzzed with anticipation, and when a couple of motorcycles flashed out of the forthcoming, creepy gates, my nipples hardened at the thrill for I was indeed in Rosewood.

"There's a couple more things you need to know before—"

My heart contracted, and I couldn't hear what Michele was saying, as another motorcycle darted out of the ugly gates. Ty's bike with him on it.

CHAPTER 23

FURORE

"**W**ipe that fucking frown off your face and get your hairy dick wet." Fort yawned, only in his boxers, scratching his balls in what remained of the kitchen. "Can't believe you spent the whole night fucking your fist in a cold bed." He grabbed himself a beer. Breakfast for champs. "But don't ya worry. I got you covered. Told all the whores to stay in. You can't wait on the bitch forever. You're fucking Prez. She ditched your ass last night. You go have some fun with another pussy. There's plenty to choose from."

"Don't call her that," I growled at my own beer, not even looking at him.

"Huh?"

"You heard me. She's *my* bitch. Only *I* get to call her that."

"Ugh, fuck this shit. I didn't throw you that motherfucking party so you can pout like a fart ass baby. You just came out of the slammer, bro. Get your cock sucked and your shit together. You don't need the trouble that girl is causing now. We need ya, and so does Rex. At least, he came. Shouldn't you be dancing off your ass that he did?"

"My shit is together, Fort. I don't need your old ass to remind me of what I gotta do. Don't forget who you're talking to."

"Sorry, Prez," he mumbled.

"And Rex only came to bitch about his fucking mother. He's still in diapers and he's giving me a piece of his shitty mind, telling *me*, his own daddy, to fuck off. I swear that boy is gonna be the end of me."

"He's a fucking prick raised by a wench, sure, but sometimes that shit is better than nothing. He hasn't talked to you in what? Fifteen years? He showed up last night, bro. Yeah, he didn't help himself to any pussy either," he rolled his eyes and threw his hands in the air like he didn't know what the fuck was wrong with us, "and he was talking shit and what not, but he showed the fuck up."

"I just didn't need that shit now. He's fucking eighteen. I thought he'd get his head out of his ass and start listening and seeing things for what they really are." I thought she would, too.

I glanced at my phone for what must have been the hundredth time, but there were no messages from her. I started to worry. What if she didn't make it because something bad happened? She and her car weren't at her place at night, either. I checked.

Or she just ditched your ass like Fort said and left town like she'd planned.

Fuck. Slamming the counter, I got off the dingy stool. "I'm going for a ride."

"C'mon," he drawled. "You're gonna look for her, aren't ya?"

I threw a glare at him and grabbed my keys. On my way out, a commotion started. Bitches were yelling, and then one of them was crying. "She hit me! I'm fucking bleeding, you bitch!"

"Ooh, a catfight!" Fort sneered, running out of the kitchen to watch the show.

Like I needed more fucking drama. My eyes rolled as I headed out. I tiptoed among the naked bodies scattered on the floor. When I reached the rubble of what used to be the lounge, there was a blonde bitch in nothing but a white tank top and a G-string hunkered on the floor, bleeding from her nose, a few of her friends gathering around her.

"I'm sorry, but you were attacking me for no reason at all."

I couldn't see who was speaking because of the swarm of angry bees blocking the view, but I'd recognize that voice anywhere.

I took one step before the blonde bitch growled, jumping to her feet, and charged forward. The swarm dispersed, and Jo was standing at the front door, a target. I was about to end this fight with one word, but Jo ducked and dodged the bitch, then grabbed her arms behind her back and twisted her wrist.

"You bitch! Prez! Fort! She's gonna break my arm!" the blonde bitch shrieked.

Fort looked at me for permission to interfere, but I shook my head. Now, *I* and my cock were enjoying the show.

"I'm not going to break anything if you just learn to use your words. How hard could that be?" Jo said, and I couldn't hold the laughter.

Silence fell in as Jo met my face. She was wearing her shades, but I knew she was staring at me as intently as I was staring at her. I couldn't explain the joy and relief filling me the second I saw her despite the rumbling rage that screamed at me to throw her over my shoulder, tie her to my bed and fuck her until she learned how to be my good girl.

"Um…okay…I'm going to—"

I didn't let her finish. I stormed toward her, wrapped my arms under her ass and carried her away from the blonde. "Help your friend," I nodded at the other bitches as I put Jo over my shoulder and hauled us to the only room that was still intact in this shithole.

"That's it? She broke my nose and my arm, Prez," the blonde whined.

I glanced at Fort to take care of it. He snorted in disapproval but went over to the bitch. He had no choice but to obey me and do his job.

"Furore, put me down," Jo yelped.

My answer was a loud spank on her hot ass. Then I squeezed it because I missed her body so fucking much. She yelped again, trying to slide out of my grip, but once we were inside, I kicked the door closed behind us and pinned her to the wall. With my hand around her throat, I grabbed her wrists and held them together above her head.

Her tits rose and fell with her catching breath, and I didn't know what to feast on first, her lips or those tits. God, the things she was doing to my body… The things I'd do to hers…

"What are you doing?" she whispered, her voice raspy, going straight to my cock.

"What the fuck are *you* doing?" She was driving me out of my fucking my mind in her absence and her presence. I'd never been that crazy about a pussy, not even when I was a fucking kid—and not even with Madeline. My whole life was about business, riding, the club and my boy. Why was I so hung up on this woman that I was ready to fuck up my whole life just to have her and keep her safe? "What the fuck are you doing to me?"

"It's your hand around my throat. What the fuck are *you* doing to *me*?"

I loved the word *fuck* from those lips and couldn't wait to hear it when she was under me, couldn't wait to see how feisty she'd become, how hard she'd scream. "Where did you learn how to fight like that?"

"It's…just reflexes."

I yanked her shades off her face and tossed them on the floor so I could see her eyes when she dared lie to my face. "Don't lie to me. Who taught you those moves?"

"They're simple self-defense moves, Furore. Every woman should know them."

"Simple my ass. You broke the bitch's nose." I squinted at her. "Are you a fucking cop?"

"What?!"

"You've always been suspicious of me. Now, it's my turn." I stared at her tits. "They sent you to spy on me? You wearing a wire?" I yanked her t-shirt off her head and dipped my hands inside the cups of her bra. The feeling of her plump tits twitched my cock hard.

"You're insane."

"Am I? I grabbed her tits out by the nipples, pinching them. "Whose fault is that?"

She squirmed with a hiss, her thighs rubbing together. "Stop groping me. I'm not a cop. Never been, never will be or have you forgotten who I am? And you can see clearly that I'm not wearing a wire."

My gaze dropped to her jeans, and I licked my lip, pushing my aching erection into her stomach. "Don't know. Maybe you're hiding it somewhere else." I rubbed the outline of the slit of her pussy on the denim up and down with one finger. "Have to make sure."

She moaned, biting her lip, hazel eyes drooping. I was itching to see her fairy ones that had enchanted me. My forehead rested on hers as my lips drew ever so closely to hers. Our breaths raced after each other, but I wouldn't kiss her yet. Not even when I was torturing myself as I was torturing her with the closeness she couldn't reach, just like she'd been doing to me, giving me hope and then running away with it. If I was going to burn, she would too.

I opened the button of her jeans and then the zipper. My fingers slipped under her panties and searched inside her folds, getting the evidence I cared for; she was soaking wet for me.

"Do you believe me now?" she murmured, pushing down on my fingers.

My gaze lifted to hers slowly, savoring her flushed tits and *come fuck me* face, as I teased the shit out of her. "There's still one place I didn't look."

Her eyes widened. "No."

I let out a quick, low chuckle. Then I yanked her jeans and panties down to her ankles in one move and flipped her in the next. I pressed her to the wall with my weight and my hand on the back of her neck. She panted a couple of moans that made my hard-on unbearable. My palm landed on her ass. God, that was definitely the sexiest ass I'd ever seen. "First, don't say no to me again." I wet my pinkie and circled her ass hole gently.

Then I, slowly, entered her. Fuck, she was so tight. Definitely a backdoor virgin. "Second, I'm gonna fuck that ass one day. That's a promise. You know why?"

"Because you…like big butts and cannot lie?"

I bit my lip on a laugh. "Not just any big butt, baby." And I didn't like her ass. I worshipped it. My gaze dropped to take her fully naked backside and bent to see the view of her pussy from where I stood. Fuck. I had to fuck her now, just like that. "But no, that's not why. I'm gonna fuck that ass to claim it. It's mine." I smacked it hard. Then I reached her pussy and gave it a swat, too, enjoying the flinch and moan her body gave. "Just like your pussy. Fucking mine."

Unbuckling my belt, I fluttered my fingers inside her. "Bend over."

CHAPTER 24

JO

I clenched hard around his fingers. The tone of his harsh, crass command and the roughness of how he was handling my body sent me spiraling into submission. I loved the pain and humiliation that came with it. The sounds my pussy was making as he pumped his fingers into me were enough proof. But I couldn't give him my full submission yet, not before I knew one more thing. "No, Laius. I don't want our first time to be like this."

"And I said you don't have a say in it anymore. Not after what you've done. You need to be punished, so you'll take my cock however I like whenever I like over and over until you learn never to ditch me ever again." He swatted my pussy again, and I'd never been more aroused. Why did I like this so much? "Time for me to teach you a lesson, Miss Meneceo."

"I understand you're upset about yesterday, but shouldn't I be, too?"

"About what?!"

"That lovely woman out there."

"*You* broke her fucking nose."

"Because she was about to attack me when she found out *I* was asking about you. She was obviously *territorial.*"

He laughed under his breath as his free hand squeezed around the curve of my waist. "You're jealous, baby girl?"

"Yes." There was no point in denying it. "You keep saying I'm yours. Doesn't that make you mine, too?" I wanted eye contact when I said that. I tilted my head to look at him, but there wasn't enough leeway. "It's the only way I'll have it, Laius," I said anyway. "I don't care about club culture or the privileges of your rank, so I want you to answer me honestly. Do you have any serious relationship with that woman or any other woman?"

"No."

A shred of relief soothed me. "Okay, but did you…"

"Did I what? Fuck her?"

"Um-hum." I swallowed, bracing for the information he was about to reveal.

"Yes."

A lump clogged my throat. "Last night?"

"You don't get to complain, you know? I just came out of prison, and my people came all the way here to throw me that party. I was supposed to be enjoying my freedom, having fun. You would have been a big part of it if you showed up. You were supposed to be there in my fucking bed, taking my cock all night and all morning. Instead, I spent the whole day being a motherfucking idiot. I waited for you, went to find you at your place, fucking twice, and left you a hundred messages. You didn't even bother to tell me you're okay."

"Look, I'm so sorry that I didn't come yesterday, but I was afraid, okay? Terrified out of my mind that I…" My voice betrayed me.

"Afraid of what?"

"Many things. One of them is this very situation. So tell me, Laius, did you fuck her last night?"

FURORE

He buried his nose in the side of my neck and then bit the tender flesh in a kiss. "You don't know how much I wanna hurt you and say yes, but I promised myself I wouldn't lie to you." His lips bit my shoulder and then I felt the scruff of his light beard traveling down on my back. His fingers left my pussy, and I almost begged for him to fill that brutal emptiness. I used the little freedom he allowed my body to turn and see him.

He was in his cut, a black t-shirt under it, crouching, his face level with my mound when I faced him. The tip of his cock poked out of his jeans, and a piece of jewelry silvered in it. I tingled with arousal at the sight of it and the anticipation of what it could be doing to my clit.

His fingers dug in my butt, squeezing, bringing me to his mouth. "I didn't touch a single woman since I've learned the smell of your cunt, Jo." He took a big whiff at my pussy, like a dog and his bitch. It was depraved and animalistic and probably the sexiest thing someone had ever done to me. Then his tongue darted inside of me, licking my wetness. "I don't think I can even if I want to. I'm addicted to you, you witch."

I trembled, hiccupping gasps, under the onslaught of his mouth, words, tongue and lips. "Laius."

He grabbed my hands and brought them to his hair, asking me with his beautiful, lustful gaze to touch him. I tangled my fingers in his hair, pulling him burying his face between my thighs, taking his tongue as deep as possible.

Those Polynesian men and their papaya eating skills had nothing on Laius Lazzarini. As if he'd given me head a thousand times before, his mouth knew where to drive me over to the edge in no time, and his tongue mastered when to flick and when to flutter.

His mischievous eyes lifted to me, needy and smoldering and intent and commanding, as if he was telling me to come with just his gaze, and I was far gone. I moaned as I came hard in his mouth, trying to keep my voice down because the people outside would definitely hear us in this torn down house. But then I changed my mind and screamed as hard and loud as this orgasm. Let them hear it. All of it. Let them know Furore was mine.

"You taste so fucking good, baby. The best thing that ever touched my mouth." His tongue lapped over me, licking and slurping. "I can't get enough. Come in my mouth one more time," he said into my pussy, and I was throbbing with need again even though I just came.

"Does that mean you're not mad at me anymore?"

"Not even close."

"Am I still getting punished?"

"Fuck yes."

"Then, first, give it to me."

His eyes dilated with more desire, and I became naughtier. "Your punishment, give it to me. I want it. All of it."

With a snarling groan, he rose, my juices staining his mouth and beard. Then he got out of his clothes and stood stark naked before me. I literally salivated as my gaze traveled down his muscular, inked body. Then my eyes widened when I saw the full hard length of him in the daylight. I'd touched him without seeing before and had a good idea of his intimidating size. Then in that holding cell, I saw part of him, but it was relatively dark, we were fighting and he didn't have his jewelry. But neither had prepared me for the real deal.

"What's the matter, baby girl?" He took my hand and guided it around his cock. Then he moved my fist all the way down to the base, where I felt not one but all three of the pieces of jewelry adorning him, and then back up to the crown. "Don't you wanna take *all* of it?"

Was it too late to take it back? I laughed at myself. While his size could be a problem with my statement, it wasn't something totally new for me. Tirone was big, too, and, with the proper care and patience, I'd learned how to take him. But Furore didn't look like he was going to be patient or careful with his plans of punishing me. And he was thicker with a plum-sized crown and more jewelry than I believed he had. "I didn't know you had three piercings." One in the crown, another in the middle of the shaft and the last at the base.

"Now, you do." He took my thumb and put it inside my mouth. Then he made me suck it ever so slowly, holding my gaze. Heat traveled down my body and centered me as his eyes darkened. There was something, almost magical, in his eyes that had the power to turn me on more than his incredible body and experienced touch. And when he made me do things to him and for him while penetrating me with his eyes, I was a puppet in his capable hands that would do whatever he said to fulfill his desires however dark or depraved.

He put his leg between mine, spreading my knees apart, and made me suck two more fingers. "Spit in your palm."

I did. "If you want me to suck your cock—
" *I'd be more than happy to.* But he didn't let me
say it. He just grabbed my wet hand and put it
back on his hardness.

He hissed under my touch, as I lubed him
with my saliva, and I'd never felt more
powerful. "I haven't had my cock sucked in
months, and I've been sporting this
motherfucking erection for over twenty-four
hours, waiting for you to take care of it." He
swiped his thumb along my lips back and
forth, and my breath snagged in my chest.
"You wrap these lips around my cock now,
I'll nut in ten seconds."

My tongue misbehaved and licked his
thumb. I wanted to suck on his fingers like he
made me suck mine. I was too empty and
needed any part of him inside me. He smirked
and let me suck. Then pre-cum glistened as I
stroked him. I smeared the liquid around him,
feasting on the arousing view. "Where are you
going to come this time?"

"You'll see," he growled, his voice strained
as my fist traveled up and down his length.
Then he dipped his hardness into my folds,
just a tiny bit, and came out. A few strokes
later, he did the same, but with his fingers
pinching my nipple.

I stopped sucking his finger with a pop. "Stop teasing me like that. Please."

His answer was more pussy teasing with his engorged cock and a spank. Slow burn. That was how he loved to torture me, making me picture things, growing with need and anticipation, while knowing that he was more than capable of delivering, of taking me to places, to levels of pleasure I hadn't reached before, and yet denying me.

"Seriously, either fuck me now or let me make you come so you can start fucking me for real."

I noticed the glow in his eyes every time I said *fuck*, and I knew he needed me as much as I needed him. But he wouldn't listen, driving me crazy with this edging technique while he added more spanking on my butt and pussy.

"God!" I was tingling with painful need, my clit pulsing in protest. "Have you not been waiting for me to *take your cock*? I'm right here and want nothing but to take it. *All* of it." I didn't care if he was going to impale me or rapture something. I needed him inside me. Now.

"You want my cock in your slutty pussy, beg for it, you little bitch."

It seemed like I still had a serious degradation kink to like this so much I was ready to go on my knees and beg like the whore I was. "Please."

"Please what?"

"Fuck me," I rasped.

It seemed that was all the control he had, because the moment I said those two words in that desperate need, he carried me and placed me on the mattress that looked fairly new compared to the dingy place, as if it was brought especially for the occasion. Then he spread me and placed his knees on either side of me.

"Do you have a condom?" I panted.

"I'm clean."

"But—"

"Nothing is gonna be between you and me. I wanna feel you around me, clenching and weeping, not a fucking bag." He pressed against me, not waiting for approval, and then he pulled my legs and wrapped the ankles around his hips and pushed inside of me.

I gasped a moan at the first entry, the ring in his crown hitting my clit instantly. He retreated a little and pushed again, getting himself deeper in me, until I felt the second hoop between my folds.

His face reddened and sweat appeared on his forehead. "You're so tight. How are you so fucking tight? Don't tell me you're a virgin, baby."

"No. But I… I didn't…" I stuttered between gasps as he didn't stop thrusting his hips. It was hard to speak when he was half way inside of me and stroking his way to make me take more of him.

"You didn't what?" He groaned.

My back arched as I cried out from the incredible stretch and the utter pleasure of his filling me. "I only lost my virginity…a few months ago."

He stilled, an alarming gleam in his eyes.

"Laius, please, don't stop. You've tortured me enough. You can't keep doing this to me. I need you. I'm right here, all yours and begging like you said I would because I fucking need you."

"Tell me you had more than one guy."

This wasn't how I imagined my first time with Furore. It had far less talking and much more fucking, and certainly didn't include any mention of my ex. "That's out of character coming from you. You sounded like the jealous possessive type. I thought you'd be happy I didn't sleep with so many men."

"I am madly jealous and possessive of you." He slammed into me hard, ripping a painful moan out of me. "That's why I'm flipping that you only had one guy and it was a few months ago. Are you still seeing him?"

"No."

"Are you fucking in love with him?" His voice was pure agony and rage.

Shit. I wasn't ready for this question, and my hesitation turned his stare into flames. "Am I a fucking rebound to you?"

"No, no! God, Laius. If you were a rebound, I wouldn't be so afraid. I wouldn't care if you were sleeping with someone else, and I wouldn't care how you saw me if you knew about..."

"Knew about what?"

Tears sprung to my eyes. "Can we please talk about this later?"

"Knew about what?" he gritted.

I looked away, guilt and shame covering me, but also frustration and despair because I truly needed Laius and he was this close to hating and leaving me. I wished I could have at least known what it felt to be his for one day. "He was my student, okay? I...I slept with my student."

"So?"

I frowned at his nonchalance. How could he not see the issue? "So it was illegal and forbidden."

"Who gives a shit? How old was he anyway?"

More shame and tears burned me. "We were supposed to wait until he was eighteen. I insisted, but…" I blew out a shaking breath. "We couldn't. He was seventeen, and I should have stopped it because I was the fucking adult, but I didn't."

"That's the worst of your shit you didn't want me to know that you ditched me yesterday for?"

"Yes, Laius. I did a horrible thing, and I can't forgive myself for it. I was terrified how you were going to see me after I told you."

"For fuck's sake. You're what? Five years older than him. That's nothing. He was fucking seventeen, and by the looks of it, not a fucking virgin. You were. So he was taking advantage of you, not the other way around. Lucky bastard. And adult my ass. If he was giving dick way before your cunt bled, he was the adult, Jo. He knew what the fuck he was doing, so don't lose sleep over him."

That was one way to look at it. Furore's justification to my crime. Michele was right, and my fears were for nothing. "Then why are you still mad?"

"Because my dick is inside you, hard and aching for you, but you're in love with some fucking kid."

"Who said I still loved him? I hesitated earlier because I didn't want to lie to you, and I hadn't confronted myself about my feelings for him lately." Ever since I saw Ty outside the club that night, I felt nothing but pain and anger. I needed to bury all my feelings aside so I could function and deal with the danger I thought I was in back then. I wouldn't let myself acknowledge any other emotions other than self-preservation and security. If I hadn't had the call with Michele, I wouldn't have confronted myself about my feelings for Laius either. "I was in love with him, yes. But it was so wrong and toxic, and it had to end one way or another."

"How did it end?"

"I don't want to talk about this." Not like this. I pointed at our bodies. "Not now."

"Is he the fucker that called you a dirty whore?"

"He never called me that. He just… He dumped me. He just took off a few months ago, and I never saw him again, okay? Well, I did see him, but he didn't, in town, twice, when all this time I thought he had to go somewhere with his family." I should probably tell him that he might have known him, too, since he was at Furore's party and his dad belonged to the dead chapter, but by the murderous look on his face I wouldn't mention Tirone to Laius. Not now, not ever. The last thing I wanted was to get Laius in trouble again…or be the reason something violent happened to Ty. I bit my lip as I gazed at his cock halfway packed inside my pussy. "Can we *please* finish what we started here?"

His eyes twitched as his breath heated between us. Then he thrust in and out of me in slow yet firm moves, getting deeper with each stroke. My mouth hung open with my moaning gasps, and my head lulled back as I begged for more of him.

"Does he make you feel like this?"

"Did, Laius, not does. But no. He didn't." Everything with Laius was familiar—the eyes, the protection, the jealous possessiveness, the anger, the big cock—yet so incredibly different. Mature. Experienced. Better. Much *much* better. Like I'd been flying economy but got upgraded to first class on this trip to a dark, sinful pleasure town.

"I'm gonna fuck him out of you until I'm all that's left."

I screamed as he upped his pace. He wasn't going to just fuck Ty out of my system. He was fucking my brains out of my head with that huge cock that felt like it did reach my skull when he slammed himself all in.

"Fuck. You feel so fucking good, Jo. So fucking good. You took all of me, in that little, tight pussy of yours. Every fucking inch. God." His groans and red, strained face while he fucked me were the sexiest things in the world. The way the metal in his cock reached all the right spots while he thrust in and out of me with skilled strokes sent me clenching hard around his swelling length.

"Jesus… You're… Fuck…" He swore as I exploded around him, screaming at the top of my lungs, letting everyone at the compound inside and outside that I was Furore's dirty whore and I fucking liked it.

He waited until I came down from the wildest orgasm I'd ever had, looking at me with some kind of awe. Then, the second I stopped clenching, he pulled out of me with a growl and came all over my face, marking it, too.

Shit. Ty had done this to me one time before, but I didn't like it at all. With Furore, I didn't even flinch as he was making it official.

I was all his.

FURORE

CHAPTER 25

FURORE

The stain of my cum on her face, hers on
my cock, all of her naked in my arms,
and yet I didn't feel she was all mine.

"I didn't think you were the cuddle and
stare type." She smiled.

"I'm not."

"Then why are you looking at me like
that?"

I was seriously wondering if she was an
actual witch. She had the body of a real
woman, with needy, naughty curves in all the
right places, but the face of an angel, so sweet
and innocent, which was now a commercial of

post-orgasmic pleasure, flushed and glowing and vulnerable, calling to me to be ruined even more. She took a big guy like me in one sitting, and that took magical talent. But above all, she made *me* addicted to her cunt even before I fucked it, sent me burning with jealousy over a teenage boy because she had feelings for him, and I was now thinking of all the ways I could erase him from her body, mind and soul so I'd be the only man for her. So she could be *all* mine. I didn't know what the fuck she was doing to me, but it was dangerous shit. "Take off your contacts."

"I'd love to. My eyes are screaming in this house with all the dust, and the contacts are making them a burning hell. But is it safe?"

"You're always gonna be safe with me, Jo."

She nodded, on her face, that smile that floored me every time, the one that sealed her fate without her even knowing it. "I trust you, but what if someone comes in?"

"You think someone can barge in on us?"

"Have you looked at those doors? If someone so much as blows on them, they'll fall apart."

"And you're okay with it? The risk of being walked in on while you're being fucked?"

"It's you who choose a place with an audience every time you touch me. I'm the poor girl who doesn't have a say in it anymore. Isn't that what you keep telling me?"

"C'mon. You fucking like it. The risk of being caught. The feeling of being watched. The thrill of being naughty. The power that you don't give a shit."

"Well, if I'm being totally honest, while I've always been discreet, living in the shadows, keeping my head low, this *openness* you offer and the power that comes with it are growing on me."

Like a disease, she gave me her smile. I was grinning like an idiot, in spite of the bubbling rage, because she made me fucking happy just by being in my arms. "You can be yourself with me. Always."

"I know. But what about with the rest of your friends?"

"I trust my crew with my life. We protect each other. They'll never hurt you. Hasn't Fort been watching out for you all this time?"

"Does he know who I really am?" she whispered, alarm lacing her voice.

"Not yet, baby, but he will. The whole crew, too. It's fucking scorching in Texas.

You can't be wearing that wig all the time. It'll give you a rash." I laughed.

Stunned, she touched her false hair. "You knew? Not even my girlfriends noticed or suspected, and they're women. How could *you* know?"

"Your girlfriends never had to buy a wig in their lives, I guess."

She stared at my hair, doe-eyed. "And you did?"

I laughed again. "For my sister. Cancer."

"Oh. I'm so sorry. Is she…"

"Alive and kicking and a pain in the ass as always. Don't worry about that little bitch. She'll outlive us all."

Her lashes fluttered. So fucking cute I wanted to eat her. "You…seem close."

"I grew up in Texas, ma'am. All families are close. Too fucking close sometimes. Sammy is the living breathing proof of it. You'd better be ready for dinner parties, barbeques and pecan pies every single Sunday. There's no escaping that. Ever."

She smiled but it didn't touch her eyes. "Laius, I—"

"Take off your wig and contacts and shut up." I knew what she was going to say, but there was no way in hell I'd accept it. I wasn't gonna leave her behind. She was coming to

Texas with me whether she liked it or not. She was mine, and I'd have her no matter what. "I'm nowhere near done with you."

She grabbed her jeans, fished out a contact case and put the fake hazels in it. Then she unfastened something at the back of her head and took the wig off. Giving me those doe-eyes, she combed through the cascades of cream blond and let them drop down her shoulders.

My cock jutted out as my hungry, mesmerized gaze zeroed in on her stunning beauty. One that matched her mother's. As if I'd taken a trip back in time, I felt like an eighteen-year-old looking at the most beautiful girl he'd ever seen, except this time she was mine and naked in my bed, ready for my taking.

"You're so fucking beautiful. Like a goddamn—"

"Please don't say it," she sighed.

"What?"

"Any faerie comparisons, jokes or innuendos."

"I was gonna say you were beautiful like an angel. A witch angel, if that's a thing."

She blushed. "Oh."

"Is that what he called you? His fucking little faerie?"

She shrugged, her lips puckered.

"You told him who you were?" I spat, flames licking me.

"He saw me naked, Laius, and he's too smart to lie to. I tried, but he kept asking questions. Eventually, I had to tell him the truth, which, surprisingly, he didn't run away from, not from that anyway. He was so protective just like you."

I wrapped my fist around her throat, and her eyes bulged. The way she was talking about him, the way her lips curved in a smile as she remembered him gnashed at me. "Don't ever compare me to another man. It won't end up well."

"What does that mean?" she rasped.

"Tell me his name." I had to know who that fucker was. I had to teach him a lesson first for hurting her and second so he'd know she was off-limits. The whole world had to know she belonged to me now. Only me.

"No."

"Why the fuck not?"

"Because...your anger...scares me."

I read her eyes, the actual fear darkening them, and my hand softened around her throat. My fingers brushed over her hair and moved a strand off her forehead. Then I kissed her there. "You can't be scared of me.

I'll never hurt you, Jo. I never hurt a woman in my whole life. If I could do something like that, that bitch Delilah would have been dead long ago. I never touched her or let anyone hurt her, and I hated her fucking guts. How could I ever hurt you when I…"

"When you what?"

My chest heaved with things I should never say or feel, so I just mashed my lips against hers. Then I flipped her on her stomach because looking at her was too much right now. It made me weak in the knees, made me want to say stupid shit that would make life as I knew it no more, shit that would ruin me before her beyond repair.

I lined my cock up with her entrance and slowly slid in. Her real hair had a curl to it I wrapped around my fist, and she whimpered softly as I pressed my face into her neck and pushed in.

She tilted her head, searching for my gaze, our gasps in unison as I gave her all of me. She was young and innocent and good, full of light I snuffed with ever touch, every stroke. And I couldn't get enough.

The best part—or the worst—was that she'd take it. She blossomed in my darkness, and she'd take it until her light was all gone. As long as she was with me, I didn't give a shit. I was that much of a selfish, cruel prick. Love was selfish and cruel. That was the only kind I knew. And I loved ruining her.

And I fucking loved her.

CHAPTER 26

FURORE

"I'd tell you to stay, but it's a dump." I kissed her forehead and cheeks as I cleaned her up with my t-shirt and helped her get dressed.

"How long are you planning on staying in San Francisco?"

"Not long. I should hit the road right away, but I'm trying to hash things out with my boy. Maybe, I'll knock some sense into his thick skull and convince him to come home with me."

"*Rex.*" She mocked.

"Yeah, Rex. What's so funny?"

"That can't be his real name. Remember how you gave me a lecture about the Italian alphabet? I've been sharpening my Italian ever since, and I know x isn't so Italian."

I snorted. "His mother gave him a fucked up name just to piss me off, so since he was three, I've always called him Rex. It was his dog's name when he was little, and he always said that would be his road name when he grew up." My jaws clenched. "Except the fucker doesn't wanna patch in. He wants nothing to do with me or the club or Texas."

"Hey," she folded her arms around my waist, "I'm sorry."

"It's not your fault."

She held on to my cut and smiled at me. "You said he was good at literature and writing, and he's in high school. English is what I teach, and he's the age of my regular students. I may understand and connect with his way of thinking better than you do. Perhaps I can do something to help."

I pulled her in and adjusted her legs so that she straddled me. "Baby, I'd love for you to meet my family, but there's no way I'm gonna let you near that prick."

She blinked, her eyes turning red, and her chin wobbled. Then she fidgeted on my lap. "Of course. I can't be trusted with children."

"Cazzo. No, baby." I held her wrists, keeping her on me so she wouldn't leave. Shit, I fucked up bad. "Oh my God, that was a joke. A very stupid joke. That's not what I meant, and he's not a fucking child anymore. Sure acting like one, but he's past eighteen."

"It doesn't matter. He's your kid, and you want to protect him from my kind."

"Jesus Christ. No, Jo. *Your* kind is too innocent to be around *his* kind...or mine for all I know. I want to protect you from him."

She sniffled, averting her gaze. "Why?"

Fuck. I wasn't planning on scaring the shit out of her too soon with talks about how fucked up Rex was. Maybe even never. At least, not until I'd won her over and had her home tucked forever in my arms with nowhere to escape. "Let's say he got my temper, and he can't control it yet. With the way that mamma's boy hates me, I don't trust him around you. I know he'll come around one day, and he'll love you because no one can hate you, baby girl. But that day ain't today."

She finally looked at me, and I wiped her wet lids. Then I kissed her like there was no tomorrow.

"I'm not scared of him," she said. "He's just a boy with daddy issues. I can relate."

I admired her courage and understanding, but it wasn't just daddy issues or a temper he had. I didn't talk about how he was messed up in the head, not even to myself, because I hoped when he was finally under my wings, away from his serpent of a mother, finding purpose and freedom in the club, knowing the true meaning of family, he'd find a way to get rid of that shit in his head.

"Allora, I am. Lo stronzo is a real charmer. Not an old fart like me. He's more your age and might steal you away from me."

She rolled her eyes with a chuckle. "Whatever. I wasn't asking to meet him, by the way. I understand how sensitive he could be if he knew you and I were… He'd never listen to me. What I was offering was simply helping you write something to him. You mentioned you wrote him letters that he never responded to."

"That would be kind of you, baby. I'd love that."

"So tell me what he likes to read."

CHAPTER 27

JO

*I*s *fucking scorching in Texas. You can't be wearing that wig all the time. It'll give you a rash. You'd better be ready for dinner parties, barbeques and pecan pies every single Sunday. There's no escaping that. Ever.*

Laius's words rang in my ears as I held tight, my breasts on his back, his engine revving under my thighs, the summer breeze fanning my face. He wanted me to come to Texas with him even if he didn't give it to me straight.

I wanted to tell him yes. I'd be happy to because that was how I truly felt. Happy. With him. But I didn't want to sound too eager, and I knew Michele wouldn't be pleased. I had to call him to convince him, already working out the conversation. *I was leaving here anyway, papà. Houston, Texas is as good as anywhere else.*

The best because that was where Laius would be, protecting me, giving me mind blowing orgasms with his massive cock and clit loving metal. Who would have known cock piercings could be so much fun?

I never touched her or let anyone hurt her, and I hated her fucking guts. How could I ever hurt you when I...

My heart fluttered when he'd said it, and every time I replayed it in my head. Again, he didn't say it straight. He chopped the words off and gave me his cock instead. But I heard it loud and clear. I saw it in his gaze. I tracked it in his groans. I felt it in his touch.

I held him tighter, rubbing my cheek against his scruff like a little cat. Did he like that? Did he even like cats? What was his favorite food? Color? Music? I found myself wondering about his trivial details and realized I knew nothing about the simple man inside the president of the Night Skulls MC. And realized how much I looked forward to finding them out.

"Do you like cats?!" I yelled over the motorcycle roar.

He grinned. "More of a dog person, baby girl!"

"Do you have any?!"

"Not at the moment, but we can get one if you want!"

A grin spread on my face, too. "I'd love that very much."

"Can't hear you, baby. What was that?"

I didn't raise my voice on purpose. I wanted to know how far he would go to make me come to Texas with him. How long it was going to take him to finally say the words he'd swallowed earlier. Or were those subtle hints and hidden declarations the best Furore could do? "Nothing! I was saying you should drop me off a couple blocks away from the building!"

"No, baby! No more of that! Everybody gotta know you're mine now!"

By everybody did he mean the Lanzas or Tirone? I didn't care because I liked both his protectiveness and jealousy equally, and I loved the fact that I was his. I never liked the concept of being a property, but the feminist in me was diminishing in a tiny corner every time he said it. *Mine.*

I kissed him on the cheek. "I love the sound of that."

He pulled over by the curb and killed the engine. I dismounted the bike, mourning the loss of the feeling of his solid abs under my palms and the sexy scent of him and his musk that would forever tickle my vagina. I hugged myself, keeping his smell on my clothes as long as possible, wishing I'd taken something that smelled of him like he'd taken my panties—again. Suddenly, he grabbed my wrist and pulled me in for a demonically passionate kiss in the middle of the street.

Dazed, eyes closed, breath knocked out of my lungs, I fanned myself when he was done. "Laying your claim here, too?"

"Just until you come to Texas with me. We own our town there. The only thing I need to lay is you on every surface I can think of."

Laughing, I opened my eyes slowly. "Who says I'm going to agree to go to Houston with you?"

"Who said I was fucking asking?"

My jaw flexed teasingly. "Well, I'll think about it."

"You're coming with me, Jo. No way in hell I'm gonna leave you here."

"Are you always that bossy?"

"Si, si. You'd better get used to it because I ain't taking no for an answer."

It was kind of hot when he threw in some Italian or Southern when he was angry. *He* was hot. Period.

I slipped my hand from his grip and ambled to the door, Fort parking my car next to the motorcycle. "I'll see you tomorrow." I waved at Laius. I wanted to invite him in, but my vagina could only take so much. He was huge, and that jewelry, while miraculous, still needed some getting used to. I was so sore. Besides, I needed to help with Rex's letter. The sooner I did it the better so we could get out of here. I wouldn't say it to Laius yet, but I couldn't wait to go live in his town.

If there was one thing I'd learned in life, it was people you loved could be taken away from you in a second, and you should never waste a second away from them or not telling them how much you loved them.

On my way in, I glanced at him over my shoulder. He was slouching against the bike, arms crossed, biceps inflated, his gaze following me all the way. He looked like he belonged on a *motherfucking* cover for a spicy romance I couldn't wait to read. "Oh, Laius, by the way…" I bit my lip, my heart thudding in my chest, "…me too."

"You too what, baby?"

I grinned with a shrug, my cheeks in a furnace. "*Me too.*" The words he'd cut off and hadn't dared say, I was saying them for him in my way.

He froze, a beautiful gleam in his gaze, and I hoped he'd understood. *I loved him, too.*

I ran up the stairs like a little girl who had just confessed her love to a boy, shy and embarrassed, afraid she'd just made a fool of herself or misread the signs. I entered the apartment, hand clutching my chest as if keeping my heart from leaping outside.

"Be still my heart." I laughed under my breath. Who knew I could fall head over heels for someone like Furore? Who knew I could be so happy again? With him, not just my pain but the shame and guilt, too faded. They became almost nonexistent. It was like a huge weight lifted off me, allowing me to breathe, to feel truly alive.

I waltzed my way into the bedroom, my smell begging me to shower after that fuck-a-thon. "All right. First shower then straight to work."

But how could I appeal to a brain like Rex's? When Laius told me the books his son liked to read, it was obvious he was messing with his father. Caselli and Torre. The Death of Santini. Oedipus. *Are you kidding me?* They were all books about patricide for God's sake. Unless Rex was a real psycho, I—

"Jo."

A loud gasp stuck in my throat, constricting it to the point I felt sick.

"Hush." Arms snaked around my waist from behind. "Don't be scared, my little faerie. It's just me."

I shuddered, my head spinning. "Ty?"

CHAPTER 28

JO

"Yes." Tirone pulled me into his body, my back to his front, his nose skimming over my neck. "Fuck, I missed you, Jo. I missed you so fucking much."

I almost passed out from the heart attack he was about to give me, but his words flared under my skin like raging pins, keeping me alert. *He missed me?! He fucking missed me?!* "How did you get in here?"

"You forgot I have a key?"

How did he get past Fort and Laius? He must have gotten in after I'd left this morning and before we returned from Rosewood. Huffing, I yanked myself away from him and twisted. I tossed my sunglasses on the bed so he could see my fury when I looked at him.

He looked exactly the same. A shiny high school alpha hole. Clean jersey and jeans. His body didn't lose any muscle weight, if something he added more to it. Perfect hair. Clean shaved. Perfect skin, no black circles under his eyes, not even a fucking pimple. No signs of sadness or sorrow. No injuries. Not a scratch. Well, except for that hole in his nose where a stupid nose ring was in place. *Piercings are more useful in cocks, asshole.*

He was standing here in my apartment, which he obviously didn't forget where it was located or lost the key to it, in my own bedroom, like he owned the place without a shred of remorse. Now. Of all the days and nights he could have returned, he chose now to show up. "What the fuck are you doing here?"

"I missed you, Jo. You're my girl."

A bitter snort ripped out of my throat. "Fuck you, Ty."

"I know you're mad at me, and you have every right—"

"Mad at you? Mad at you, Ty? Oh my God. Mad is when you have a fight or get stood up or even catch someone cheating. You disappeared on me without a word. For two fucking months. And now you had the audacity to come back just like that saying you missed me, calling me your girl?

"Do you have any idea how many times I called and left you messages begging you to tell me if you were okay? Do you have any idea how worried I was? I thought something happened to you, Tirone. I was going out of my mind, trying to find you. I searched for you at hospitals and police stations. I even risked everything and went to your house. Do you have any clue how horrible and stupid I felt when I found out you were here all this time, safe and sound?"

"Jo, please, listen to me."

"No." I drew a hand over my eyes before any tears slipped away. "You can't just come and go whenever you like. You can't ghost when you want and talk when you like and demand I listen."

He stepped toward me, his hands reaching for my face.

I raised a finger between us. "Don't even think about touching me. You know what? Just…just get out."

"You have to listen to me. You have to let me explain."

"I don't have to do anything with you or for you. There was a time when I'd have given anything to see you again, to have you here and let you explain why the fuck you did that to me, but now…" I chuckled without humor. "I don't care anymore. Whatever it is, it doesn't matter. Get out, Tirone."

He just stared at me, hurt in *his* eyes. Like he had any right to be the wounded one here. I stepped out of the room, gesturing at the front door so he'd take a hint.

"I lied to you," he said. "About my father. He's not dead."

What? I stopped in my tracks, but then I shook my head in disbelief, reprimanding myself for allowing any kind of feelings toward whatever he had to say or do. How could I even believe anything he'd say? He could be lying through his teeth for all I knew. There was no chance I could trust him again. "I told you I didn't want to hear it. Whatever it is. It's over, Tirone. You and I are over."

"Don't say that." His voice came from a dark place, not pain or regret or fear.

How he thought he still had any power over me or control over our relationship, how he still felt possessive of me that he could just come back and expect me to resume things where he left off like my feelings didn't have any right to change, how he thought he could intimidate me with his dark side to manipulate me into coming back to him infuriated me even more. "Oh, I will. You know why? The second you decided to walk out on me without even a goodbye, you gave up every right to be standing here now, telling me what or what not to do. You gave up everything related to us. So I'm telling you again, *us* doesn't exist anymore, Ty. You and I are over."

I walked toward the door, but I was dragged backwards by his strong grip. "No!" My heels dug in the carpet as my arms reached for anything I could use to stop him. He lifted me in the air before I grabbed anything and hurled me on the bed. Then he pinned me down with his weight.

"What the fuck are you doing?!" I shouted.

He held my wrists above my head despite my struggle. "Reminding you who owned you."

"Get the fuck off of me, Ty. Now."

He unbuttoned his jeans. "Not before I get back what's mine or have you forgotten, Jo? You made a promise to me. You belong to me. But it's okay. I'll make you remember."

"You're insane. Get off of me. I don't belong to you. Not anymore. Get off of me, you asshole!"

"There's no such a thing. You're *my* little faerie. Always will be." He lowered his jeans enough to free his cock. Then he tried to take off mine. I writhed hard, my legs flailing behind him as I slid my body back so that my knee would reach his balls.

"Why are you fighting me, Jo? I know you're angry, but I'm back, and I'll make it up to you." His mouth approached mine, but I jerked my head away. He still kissed my cheek. "You're my girl, and I love you."

"I said I'm not yours anymore," I seethed.

His eyes darkened with familiar rage. Then he inhaled me. "What's that smell you reek of?"

Tirone's darkness was dangerous, yet I knew how to handle it. Fuck, at some point, I even craved it. That was why I was beneath him against my will, but I wasn't truly afraid. Somehow I knew I could fight him off one way or another. But when he smelled Laius on me, that was when real horror crept up my body.

"That's none of your business. Now, get the hell out of my apartment and never show me your face again."

He wiped his mouth and stared at me for a second. The next he tore my pants down, exposing my pussy. I screamed at him, but he choked me. "Where the fuck are your panties, Jo?"

My eyes teared up, but I kept my mouth shut. Just like I wouldn't tell Laius about Ty to protect them both, I would never tell Ty about Laius.

His face contorted as if he was about to cry, but I wouldn't be fooled by it. I used the tiny opportunity of his loosening up his grip and pushed myself back. Then my knee smacked his balls. As he bent, groaning, I hit him in the ribs, and then crawled and tripped out of the bed.

I pulled my pants up to run out of the apartment, but he barreled down on me, bringing me back to the floor. His ironclad arms fully immobilized me. "Do you not remember what happened the last time some fuck tried to touch you?"

I did. At a bar we went to on one of our trips out of town, one guy tried to grope me, thinking I was alone. Ty beat the shit out of him, took his wallet, threatened to tell his wife and register him as a sex offender in ten different states. Then Ty broke the guy's hand.

I thought it was one of the nicest things someone did for me.

Click.

My heart thrashed at the sound. The memory of the night I'd lost my mother flashed behind my eyes because I'd heard a similar sound back then. That click belonged to a gun. Was that *my* gun?

"I'm sorry, Jo. It's not your fault. It's mine. I should've been here to protect you, to stop that piece of shit before he took something that didn't belong to him. But it's okay, baby. I'm here now. I'll fix it. It won't be just his hand I'll break. I'll kill the son of a bitch."

"The fuck, Ty? Are you crazy?" I inclined my neck toward him, and I glimpsed the gun barrel poking from his hand, knowing beyond doubt it was real. It was mine. "Put the gun down."

"You have to tell me who it is so I can make things right."

"No, Tirone. You can't do this. Oh God." I began to sob. How had I ever been in love with someone as dark and dangerous and psycho as Tirone? How had I been pretending he wasn't deeply disturbed and in dire need of professional help? Obviously, I needed the same for loving him and his darkness.

How did I get myself and Laius in this situation?

I had two choices. Try to fight, just like I did with the club whore, using everything Michele had taught me to defend myself since that night he saved me from the men of my father's wife. Or give up my life for the man I loved. Option one—if I didn't get myself shot dead—would buy me some freedom, but then what? Tirone wouldn't just let me go. He'd come after me, and that would lead him to Laius. Then one of them would be dead and the other would be in prison for life. Same thing if I asked Michele for help. Blood. Tirone would be dead. Perhaps Laius, too.

I couldn't live with myself if Tirone died because of me. I cared about him still, as my former student and as a man I used to love. He was young, and with the right help, he had his whole life ahead of him. I couldn't let Laius get hurt because of me either. I loved him, and he had a son to live for.

I, on the other hand, was unwanted from the day I was born. I brought nothing but trouble to the people who loved me. "Listen, Ty. The other guy at the bar tried to touch me against my will, and you made him pay for it. This time, it's different. I wanted it. I fell in love with another man and gave him myself.

It was all *my fault*. If you have to kill someone, then kill me."

He flipped me on my back, scowling at me. "How could you say that?"

"It's the truth. You left me. Still, I waited for you. I thought you loved me like I loved you. I thought you meant it when you said I was yours. Until I saw you that night at Belle View and realized how much of an idiot I was. So I fell in love with someone else."

"Shut up."

"No, I won't. I don't love you anymore, and I love him, you know why? Because you're just a boy, and he's a real man. He knows how to take care of a woman."

"I said shut up."

"Shoot me, Ty. Do it. I betrayed you. I let another man fuck my pussy, *your* pussy, and I fucking loved it. If you're a man, shoot me. Now."

He shook his head, growling. "No. No!" He pressed the gun to my temple. "How could you say that?" He slid it along my cheekbone and then down to my neck. I closed my eyes, taking a deep breath, knowing it was my last. A shiver took over me that I could barely control. Fear, self-preservation, or just desperation, I didn't know or care. My life meant nothing. It was a trivial price to pay to save the person I loved.

As tears spilled down my face, I said goodbye to Laius in my head.

"How could you say that?" The cold barrel left my skin. "You know I can never hurt you, Jo. No matter what you do, I'll never hurt you, baby. You're my little faerie."

His breath fell on my lips. My eyes snapped open as he took my lips between his. "No." I pushed him off my face. "I'm telling you I'm in love with someone else. You kill me now or you fucking leave me be."

"You're smart enough to know that's never gonna happen. I can't live without you, Jo." The back of his hand brushed against my face. "I forgive you, baby. Always. That twat you call a man, though," he smiled darkly, "will still be dead."

"No, Ty, no," I sobbed.

"Hush." He pulled down my pants again. "Now, where were we?"

"If you touch me, I swear to God I'll kill you myself."

He pressed the gun on my mound, and my heart dipped. "You just fucked another man. You think I'll just dive in after him?" He sighed, shaking his head. "I have to clean you up."

"I'm not dirty, Tirone. If I ever was, it was because of you. You treated me like a dirty whore and dumped my ass, leaving me to rot in fucking shame and guilt and hate. I'm proud of being his girl now, and I'll hold his cum inside me as long as I can."

His jaw twisted while he gave a low snarl. Then he put the barrel inside my pussy. My eyes widened at him, and I forgot how to breathe. "What the fuck?"

"Since when do you swear like a biker, Jo?"

My heart forgot how to beat, too. Holy shit, did he know?

"Did you really think I just left you?" He pushed the gun barrel inside me and then out, fucking me with it, stopping my heart with every terrifying, humiliating thrust. "Here's the thing, baby. I disappeared because my piece of shit father isn't dead like I told you. Mom left him years ago because he abused her. She was afraid he was going to abuse me, too. But the day I disappeared, he came to our house, drunk, and attacked my mother. He almost killed her. I stood up to him, and he attacked me, too. She called the cops in time. Who knew what would have happened if they hadn't caught him?"

He watched me gasp as he entered me with a weapon, and then his eyes sparked with arousal as he watched the barrel glisten with my juices and what remained of Laius's cum. "He threatened me that day, Jo. He threatened to hurt me because I helped my mother. The only way he could hurt me was through the people I loved. Mom and you. I had to stay with her all the time to protect her, at least, until I knew he was behind bars. At the same time, I was afraid he was gonna find out about us and hurt you, baby. He's a criminal with ties to the mob. What if he found out who you really was?" He pushed the gun deeper, violating me. "I had to pretend I didn't know you, Jo. I had to pretend I didn't care about you only to protect you, baby. But I was never gonna leave you. How could you think I would?"

I didn't know what to say or even feel, so I just cried. Maybe if I hadn't met Laius, maybe if I hadn't had a literal gun in my vagina, there would have been a chance I believed him and even forgiven him. I'd have seen what he'd done as a noble sacrifice and loved him even more.

But why did he not just tell me the truth back then? We had a burner phone he could have answered once to explain. That was all it would have taken to keep me from the heartache and worry. Instead, I was being forced to listen to his story, which was supposed to make me forgive him, that could be nothing but lies, while being fucked with a gun. He was *cleaning me up*, scraping my pussy out of another man's cum with a fucking loaded gun.

"I'll never leave you, little faerie. You're the love of my life. You understand me. You love me. So do I. Even when I had to go away, I kept my eye on you when I could. At first, I had to stay away completely, but when he was sentenced to a couple of years behind bars, I checked in on you. I knew you got that job at the Arena. I knew you were still at the school. I even saw you at Belle View, but I couldn't talk to you. I couldn't be seen with you without risking your life. Can you imagine how hard that was for me? To be this close to you and never be able to even say hi?" His whole face darkened. "Then I saw you this morning in Rosewood…"

"Ty…please stop."

"Stop what?" He pointed at the gun. "This?"

"Yes. Please."

"Not until you come, *Miss Meneceo*."

"What?" How could I fucking come with a loaded gun scratching inside my vagina about to blow my insides up any second?

"Remember when *I* called you Miss Meneceo in bed? I thought that was our thing. But you just had to fall for another student. In fucking prison."

Tears flooded out of me. Tirone knew about Laius, and I didn't know what to do to protect the man I loved from my psychotic ex. "How did you know all those things? And what were *you* doing in Rosewood?"

"Well, the part where my father is Night Skulls is real. They were having a party, which I'm sure you knew about, and I was invited because I'm kind of legacy. It's a club thing. I'm sure your new boyfriend told you."

"He's not my boyfriend."

"Oh, Jo. He made you become a liar, too?" He pushed the gun even deeper that it felt as if lodged in my throat. "You know when I didn't see you last night I was so happy. I thought my doubts were nothing but that, doubts. I thought you were still waiting for me, and I was counting the seconds until I came back and told you everything, knowing you'd understand because you had a shitty father, too, and then you'd forgive me and everything would be just the same. But..." He sighed a moan. Then he dipped his fist inside my now loose wig and fisted the back of my hair, staring at me angrily. "Come like you came for him this morning." He pushed the gun in and out of me faster, hurting me, punishing me, fucking me. "Come."

"I can't," I whimpered.

"Then how about I use my cock instead? That will do the trick. Always did."

"No."

"You don't seem to understand me, baby. You will break up with Furore, and you will give me back my pussy if you want him to stay alive. Otherwise, you'll leave me no choice but to wipe that motherfucker off the face of earth and fuck you on top of his fucking corpse, in front of his whole gang if I had to."

My eyes squeezed. A few months ago, I'd have thought that was hot. I liked it when he made those jealous threats. I loved it when he was possessive of me. Listening to them now, knowing they could become more than empty threats, knowing it was Laius he was going to hurt, curdled the blood in my veins. "Do you think if you kill him I can be with you again?"

"Maybe not at first, but you'll come around. You know why? Because nothing matters but you. You're everything, and I'll do anything to make you mine. I don't care if you hate me as long as you're with me, and with time, my beautiful little faerie, you'll learn to love me again." He bent over me, and his forehead rested on top of mine. "What's it gonna be, Jo? You'll come back to me, and no one needs to get hurt? Or I'll be using this gun on something far uglier than your sweet pussy?"

CHAPTER 29

FURORE

Mtoo. Her voice played on repeat every second of my ride back to Rosewood, and for hours later, I could hear nothing else but those sweet two words. *Me too.* I was an idiot for not saying it back to her right on the spot and for not saying it at all when I was about to. She heard it, though. She felt it, and she said it back.

I wanted to call her right away. Fuck, I wanted to go back, crawl into her bed and say it to her loud and clear while I was buried deep between her thighs. But I needed to give the girl some distance or she'd get tired of me real fast.

My phone rang, and I wished it'd been her. It was my VP, though. "Molar, bro."

"You gotta come back, y'all. I can't hold your sister off anymore. She won't shut up about taking a plane by herself to come down to you. She's screaming at me at the hospital, driving me nuts."

I chuckled. "Put her on the phone."

"Can't. Chemo started already."

"Okay. I'll call her tonight and tell her I'm coming back this week. How is she?"

"Kicking butt. Missing your old ass, though. When you say this week what day exactly is that, Prez?"

"Look, I wanna come home right away, but I'm trying to hash things with Rex."

"You think you can get that done in a week?"

I sighed. "Well, I'm giving it one last shot. If it works, it works. If it doesn't…"

"I didn't wanna say something now, but you gotta know Armando Lanza landed in town an hour ago."

"The fuck? Why didn't you tell me right away?"

"Because I'm taking care of it until you return. Did he request a meet?"

"No. Is it just Armando?"

"For now, I reckon."

"Okay. I'll shift gears and come as fast as I can. I'll send Fort over right away. Keep me posted." Fuck. I hung up and called Fort.

"Prez, I'm dropping Jo from the school. We're down at her place."

"Put her on the phone."

"Laius."

I picked something in her tone that set me on edge. "What's wrong, baby?"

"Nothing. I was just sorting a few things at the school. You know saying goodbye to my friends and getting my reference letters."

Hadn't she done that already? She was planning on leaving the city weeks ago. "Baby—"

"I finished the letter, by the way. I gave it to Fort, and he'll give it to you."

"What fucking letter?"

"For Rex. I thought if you gave it to him soon enough, and hopefully, he'd respond in your favor, we can start our road trip to H-town."

I should be over the moon now that she was agreeing to come home with me, but something was off. My instincts never lied to me. "That's great news, baby girl. Thank you so much for doing this. I'll send the letter right away, but I won't wait for Rex to respond."

"What are you talking about?"

"Shit is happening back home, and we need to get going. How soon can you pack?"

"Um...give me a couple of days."

"How about I come help, and we leave tonight?"

She paused. "If you come over, we won't get any packing done." Her laugh was void of humor.

"What's wrong, baby? Are you having second thoughts?"

"No. Don't be ridiculous. I was only teasing when I said I was going to think about it. I want nothing but to go with you, Laius. Listen, how about I just pack my essentials while you go talk to your son and we can send for the rest of my things later?"

Okay, maybe I was worried for nothing. She wasn't having second thoughts, and I was being an idiot. I just never felt like this about anyone, never wanted any woman as much as I wanted Jo. To want something that much meant to be scared shitless to lose it, and I'd forsaken fear a long time ago to become the man I was. My love for her was changing me, and it scared me even more. "Sounds like a plan. I'll pick you up around midnight."

"Laius, I…" Her voice wavered.

"Hold that thought until I see you. I want to be looking in your eyes when you say it. I want you to be looking in mine when I say it. And I want to say it first. But for now…*me too*, baby."

Her breath rustled, and she sounded like she was holding her tears. "*Sounds like a plan.*"

"Baby, is there something else you want to tell me?" I couldn't help that fucking feeling that something was wrong.

"Just that Fort is looking at me funny like I were some sort of alien."

"Ain't no alien but a witch like Prez says. You put a magic spell on my bro," Fort said.

I snorted. "All right, get your ass over here and give me that letter. Jo, do your thing, and I'll see you in a few hours."

I texted Molar, telling him the plan had changed. Fort wouldn't be the only one coming home tonight.

CHAPTER 30

JO

"The whole point of my going to the school was to take Fort away from the area and you can leave without being seen. What are you still doing here?" I asked Tirone, who was still in my apartment, sitting in a corner in the dark like a creep.

"Staying at my girl's place for the night. You used to be happy when I did. You couldn't fall asleep without me, Jo. You told me I scared away the nightmares."

"Until you turned into one."

He inhaled deeply as he rose from the chair. I flipped on the light switch and flinched when he came closer. "Are you literally scared of me?" he asked in disbelief.

"I want you to leave, Ty."

"Why are you still mad at me? Why can you not see that I only left to protect you and came back as soon as it was safe to be by your side again?"

You put a gun in my vagina and threatened to kill the one person that made me happy. "You came back for you not for me. You only reappeared in my life when you saw me being happy with someone else. You couldn't stand it because you're sick."

A muscle ticked in his jaw. "You're not happy with him. Any feelings you have for this man comes from your anger at me. Once it's gone, you'll see I'm the only one you love. The only one that can make you truly happy, not give you the illusion of it."

"If I told you I was no longer mad at you because I genuinely don't care about your abandonment anymore, if I told you my feelings for Furore were real and so was the happiness I only felt with him, would you change your mind and let me go?"

He placed his palms on either side of my face, and my stomach tied in a knot of bile.

His thumbs stroked my cheeks as he bent and laid a kiss on my neck. I shuddered at the touch I used to melt under yet now made my skin crawl. Then he looked at me with a smirk. "Never, little faerie."

My eyes squeezed shut as pain seared me. Was this my destiny? A lifetime of punishment and pain and fear just for falling for the one person I should never have had?

"Did you do as I said?" he asked, the dark notes in his voice evident.

"I told him I was going away with him tonight and sent Fort away. Furore will be here at midnight, where he'd wait for me only to find out I was long gone." I fought my tears. "Then he'd see that note you made me write that told him you and I got back together."

"Good girl."

My skin crawled at the two words I loved the most. I didn't want to hear it from him ever again. Only from Furore. My eyes roamed at the boxes I hadn't either unpacked or finished packing since the time I was about to leave the city. Only now there were fully packed. "What did you do?"

"Surprise," he sang.

I batted my eyelashes in confusion. "You packed for me?"

"Yes. And the moving truck is on the way." Excitement dripped from his tone. "You get dressed, we'll pop quickly at my place to pack a backpack, then we'll be off on our way, baby, just like old times. I promise it'll be the ride of our lives."

My heart felt like ice. "What are you talking about?"

"We're moving out. Together. Did you really think I was gonna let you go by yourself even for a little while? Are you silly? I just got you back, and I'm never leaving you ever again."

My head buzzed, and my vision blurred like I was about to pass out. "Tirone, this wasn't the plan. We agreed that I'd break up with Furore in this hideous way so he'd hate me and stop trying to be with me, and only *I* would go away for a little while to convince him I did run off with you. You didn't say anything about coming with me."

"How stupid do you think I am, Jo?" His excitement vanished, and all was left was his dark side. "Not stupid enough to make believe once you step out of that door, you'll come back to me. I know you're planning to run away. I can't let that happen, baby."

I swallowed, the muscles around my heart squeezing. "What about your mother and school? It's starting soon. You can't waste another year."

"Schools are everywhere, and I'll find a way to convince Mom to come live wherever we're gonna be."

"What about work? My teaching job, if I still can get one somewhere else, can't support us both."

"Baby, have you forgotten who I am? I'm Tirone Wisely. My stepdad is loaded. Don't worry about money at all. I got it all covered."

"How, Tirone? Do you have any idea where we're even going?"

"Yup. But I'm not gonna tell. It's gonna be a surprise."

I wiped my hands over my face, many times, trying to stay conscious and to wrap my head around all this, around the trap I fell right into and had no clue how to get out of. "Wow. You had it all figured out, huh?"

"I'll do anything for you, Jo. This is me keeping my promises. I'm your man, and I'll take care of you, make up for all the mistakes I made. We can be together out in the open. You're no longer my teacher, and I'm eighteen. Nothing is gonna stop us now."

I plopped down on the next chair because my feet could no longer carry me. He squatted in front of me. "Baby, you okay?"

I was stuck in an obsession as dark as hell with no way out. "I…I don't feel so well. I'll go to the bathroom."

"Let me come with you."

"The fuck, Tirone? I can't get some privacy even in the bathroom?"

"You can have all the privacy you want. I'm not holding you captive. I just wanted to help in case you were gonna be sick. You know, hold your hair or something."

I staggered out of my seat. "Thanks, but I'll manage." Locking the bathroom door behind me, I whimpered. I couldn't live like this for the rest of my life. Something had to be done.

I took off my wig fast, my stomach acting up. Nausea hit me hard, and I emptied my guts in the toilet. I washed up and looked for something to ease the nausea and anxiety in the medicine cabinet.

Knock! Knock!

My whole body jumped, and I almost fell off my feet. Shit. I needed to pull myself together if I had any chance to survive this.

"I'm worried about you, baby. Please let me in. Let me take care of you."

The genuine care in his voice messed me up. Every word he said no matter how sweet came from a dark place, but he believed it was all real. Fuck, *I* believed it was real. In his twisted way, he still cared about me. In my fucked up way, I wanted him out of harm's way. How could he still sound so sweet? How could I care about him when he'd just ruined my life?

"Jo?"

"I'm fine. I'm coming out in a minute."

When he was assaulting me, all I could think of was ways to get him off me without accidentally setting the gun off. I could have easily attacked his eyes, and then used the gun on him, yet I couldn't do it. I was too scared to permanently hurt him.

Now, after I'd learned his awful plan, the only viable solution to this whole situation was to call Michele. He'd know how to scare Ty off and get me away from him, except Michele Pagani was a made man. His solution was painted red. The odds of Ty making it out alive were slim, and my stupid heart wouldn't accept it.

What did that say about me?

Knock! Knock! Knock! Knock! "Please let me come in."

My fists clenched as I swore at him under my breath. Then I opened the door. "I said I was coming out in a minute. Here I am." I moved past him and glanced at the bed where

one of my outfits was splayed on the sheets.
"I see you chose my clothes for me."

"If you want something else—"

"It'll do. How about you let me change so
we can get out of here?"

His hands fondled my waist. "You're shy of
me now?"

I fucking slapped him. I couldn't take this
anymore, and my palm rang across his face.

"What the fuck, Jo?"

I slapped him on the other cheek. "If you
think you're gonna see me naked or lay a hand
on me any time soon, you're delusional."

He fumed, his chest heaving, his face
crimson with my fingers marking it. He
looked like he was about to pounce, but he
just closed his eyes and nodded. "I get it. Of
course, you need time. I'm sorry. I just miss
you."

"Close the door on your way out."

When he did, I locked it and changed.
Then I gathered my personal belongings in a
purse. I glanced at the note I'd left Laius, tears
threatening to spill. "I'm sorry. I hope one day
you'll forgive me and understand I did this for
you," I whispered, lifting my chin so I
wouldn't cry, and headed out of the room.
"I'm ready."

Ty was on the phone, his fingers pinching the bridge of his nose. Then he hung up and wiped under his eyes. Was he crying?

Tirone wasn't a man afraid of his tears, and I hated it when he did that because…I was a sucker for it. He tore me apart every time I saw his tears, and I couldn't feel anything soft for him right now. "Who are you talking to?"

"Mom. I was asking her to get my things ready for me to pick it up so we won't be late. It's almost eight, and the movers will be here at nine."

"Did you…tell her about me?"

"I told her everything this morning, but, for your safety, I didn't give her your name or told her you were my teacher. Don't worry. We have her blessing."

I was neither worried nor did I care about her blessing. That ship had sailed weeks ago. But I saw a little window of opportunity here. "Ty, if you're that attached to your mother, you have to stay with her. You're her only son, and both of you went through hell with the attack. You can't just take off. We can work out a different plan that doesn't involve—"

"Nice try, but you can't get rid of me that easily." He grimaced, and I cursed my luck. "I wasn't crying because I was leaving Mom. I'll see her again soon, and she'll be fine with my stepdad. My prick of a father can't hurt her anymore. I'll make sure of it. I was crying because I never thought there would come a day when you wouldn't let me touch you. I was crying because I screwed up and almost lost you, Jo."

I hated that my first reflex was to hug him, and that tears pricked my eyes. Ty was my first everything, and a few weeks ago, he was my only everything. Despite what he'd done, the things that connected and bonded us, the things that attracted me to him and eventually made me fall in love, the dark before the light, were pulsing in him. The part of me that loved him to death was still there and couldn't be denied.

That was a weakness I couldn't afford.

"Well, you're here, and so am I. Let's see if you can keep your promises this time."

He strode toward me and kissed my hand. "I will. You'll see." His gaze spied the purse. "What's in there?"

I opened it for him. "My contacts, medicine for the road, water. It's late, and I don't know how far we're going. I like to be prepared for anything."

He just smiled and took it from me. "It's heavy. Let me carry it for you."

"Thanks."

He ushered me and the suitcases out. Then he loaded them in my car and drove to his house.

"What are you going to do about your bike?" I asked.

"It's coming with the boxes. I know how much you love it. We can still get our rides off with the sunset, baby."

"Great." I pressed my thumb against the top of my stomach and moaned.

"Something wrong?"

"It's that nausea again. I should take another pill. Good thing I got them all."

"Sure." He reached for the backseat and brought me my purse.

I went through it and popped in a pill. But a few seconds later I felt really sick. "Ty, pull over. I think I'm gonna be sick."

"Shit. Okay." He stopped the car and climbed out. The he opened the door for me. What a gentleman.

I bent over by the curb, holding on to the purse, and vomited. When I was done, I rummaged through the purse again. "Ty, can you help me find a tissue?"

"Sure." The second he dug his head inside the purse, I stuck a syringe in his neck. The actual thing I was looking for. "What the f…"

He couldn't continue, falling unconscious in my arms.

I laid him gently on the backseat and drove off. Once I found a place away from traffic, I left his sedated body and the whole city of San Francisco behind me.

CHAPTER 31

JO

I stared at my burner phone for almost an hour as I hunched down in a motel room near Utah. A desperate voice nagged me to call Laius, telling me I was doing us both no good, and I should have just told him the truth. If I'd had learned anything from what Ty did in the name of saving and protecting me, it was it didn't work. It only ruined us beyond repair.

But I wasn't Laius. I didn't have anger issues that made me go rampage, beating people around or worse.

Another voice, more sensible, urged me to call Michele. Chicago, under the protection of Don Sebastiano Bellomo's personal bodyguard, was the most logical choice to go for when I had a psychotic ex that I was certain wouldn't stop looking for me, and a very angry boyfriend that probably wanted to murder me for what I'd done to him.

Except I didn't want to go back to this life of blood and hate.

It didn't seem I had much of a choice, though. It was better than the alternative, and I shouldn't judge. Not after I was willingly going to live in Texas with Furore, the president of the Night Skulls. He didn't exactly preach at a church. I wasn't oblivious to the club activities, and Michele had confirmed them. They had business with the Mob and the cartel. Going back to Chicago had the exact same risks I'd accepted to take to be with Laius.

But he won't be there. Why take such risks to be all alone?

God, I was tired of overthinking. My head felt as if set on fire. "I'm twenty-three for God's sake. This shouldn't be my life. What the fuck should I do?"

Lights flickered through the curtains and spilled into the room. Headlights. Quietly, I grabbed the gun and held it as I peeked from the curtains. It was four in the morning, I was on the run, and every light, sound and movement freaked me out.

Through the window, I glimpsed a black sedan sliding into the parking lot, and a couple came out of it. Okay. False alarm.

However, I refused to live in that kind of fear any longer. I'd been hurt, lost and alone. Furore's eyes always screamed at me a sacred promise, "No more, never again." I believed him, and I loved him, but I was broken by fear. No matter how hard I tried, I didn't know how to be whole. How could I let him in my life when I was nothing but sharp pieces threatening to cut and stab and hurt anyone who dared come close?

I made up my mind. I put the gun on the side table and started to dial Michele's number.

Bam!

The phone dropped when I gasped, jumping off the bed as silver lights pooled inside the room. I grabbed the gun as two figures entered through the broken down door. I twisted and aimed at one of them. *Bang!*

"Son of a—"

Did I hit or miss? Fuck. I didn't have time to panic or wonder. My finger hit the trigger again, but the second person held my arm up and put a bag over my head. "No! No!" I kicked as hard as I could, firing without aim; I couldn't see anything.

"A little help here. She's feisty as fuck," he said as he twisted my wrist and dropped my gun on the floor with a thud.

"The bitch shot me. Why didn't he say she had a gun?"

"What?! Who's he?! Who are you?!" I kept kicking at the shins of the man holding me, elbowing him as well.

Footsteps approached me, and a something pricked my neck. No. Did they just drug me like I did with Ty? As my head spun, and blackness surrounded me, I realized karma was a bitch, and I was fucked.

CHAPTER 32

JO

A thousand-pound headache split my skull in half. In a haze, I willed my eyes to open. What the hell happened to me? And who were those two men who took me?

Could it be Step Mommy Dearest? Or had the Lanzas finally figured it out and collected their prize? The latter would explain why I was still alive.

Taking in the surroundings, the only thing I could make out through the drowsiness and the fact that my body could barely move was sunlight. How long was I out? Why could I not move?

I snapped my eyes open, an annoying yet consistent buzz in the background, and a little spike of adrenaline nudged me up. My body lifted off the bed I was in just a little before I realized I was on my stomach and my wrists were cuffed to the bed. "Fuck!" I yanked at the chains. "What the hell did you do to me?! Who did this?!"

Panic had me on full alert mode. I looked down and a sliver of relief washed over me when I saw my shirt on. The buzz stopped, and another person's breath hit my ears. Panic turned into sickening dread at the coldness of my lower body and the tightness around my ankles. I was naked from the waist down, and my ankles were restrained, too. "No. No. Fuck you." Crying, cuffs rattling, I twisted, kicking and screaming, to see who the fuck did this to me, to no avail. "I'm going to kill you. Whoever you are I'm going to fucking kill you! What did you do to me? What the fuck did you do to me?!"

"Easy, baby girl. Don't hurt yourself."

I froze at the voice. Then I let out a long breath. "Oh my God. I'm going to kill you, you son of a bitch. You did this?"

"Yes. So sit still until I finish."

"Finish what?"

The buzzing returned, and then something sharp tickled my buttock. "Is that… What the fuck, Laius? Are you giving me a tattoo without my consent? On my ass?!"

"*My* ass. It's *my* ass, Jo. Since you seem to forget, I reckoned a reminder was in order so you'd always remember."

Sobbing, I twisted my neck again so I could see him. I was enraged by his actions—he was branding me for fuck's sake—but I'd missed him and needed to see his face. He wouldn't give me that much, though. He was hurt, and he had every right to be. "Stop, Laius. I know I hurt you, but that doesn't give you the right to kidnap me. To cuff me to bed like that and fucking mark me."

He didn't speak, and the needle didn't stop pricking my skin.

"Goddamn it, Laius. Fuck this shit. Are we in Houston?"

"Yup."

"How did you find me?"

"A GPS tracker on your car. Fort did it early on when he was watching you."

"Oh my God."

"What were you doing in Utah? And where the fuck was that punk ass kid you ran off with?"

I just shook my head.

The buzzing and the needle pricking stopped. Then a photo capture sound ripped the silence. His footsteps approached from the side. His frame shadowed out the bright sun. His beautiful face numbed my aches and disturbance for a second, but the blame in his gaze set them ablaze. He flashed his phone at me with a photo on the screen.

Property of Furore. On my big wrinkly butt.

My fists and eyes squeezed. Violated was an understatement of how I felt, and rage was dulling any kind of guilt I was feeling for hurting him. "You fucking branded me."

"You fucking ran away with a piece of shit kid who dumped your ass and left you hating yourself after you told me you were moving in with me. After you told me you were mine."

"You don't know anything."

"Your piece of crap note was pretty elaborate, Miss Meneceo."

I rattled my chains, the fog from the drug his men used on me fading, and I was fully aware of the pain pulsing on my ass from the tattoo. "Get me out of these cuffs."

"Not until you tell me what the fuck happened."

I yanked hard at the restraints, my wrists, ankles and naked butt burning. "Get me out and put my pants back on!"

Suddenly, he was on top of my back, subduing me with his strength. His arms were tight on my waist and his scruff was scratching my chin. "When will you learn that fighting me gets you nothing but fucked? Is that what you want, baby? To get fucked?"

My lips curled under my teeth because in this situation, where I was kidnapped, cuffed, half naked and branded against my will, while a man was threatening to fuck me, I wanted to fucking smile. How could I like that? How could my pussy become wet when I was vulnerable like that?

He cupped my pussy and let his fingers in. I trembled when he found the evidence of my shameful arousal. "I'll take that as a yes."

"Laius…no."

He chuckled at my lie, his hand moving at my lower back. Then something clinked, which I assumed was the buckle of his belt, and then a zipper came undone. He gave my pussy a swat before he pressed his hardness against my opening. "Lift those hips for me, baby girl."

When I didn't move, his strong grip did it, and then he spanked me. "Bad girl."

I swallowed, clenching. I bit my lip on another smile. "Is this even your bed?" It smelled like him, and it added fuel on my desire for him.

"What dumb question is that?" He entered me with a tight groan. "This is my room at the compound."

The front jewelry of his cock hit my clit immediately, and the way he began to fill me pushed away every other feeling. When Laius fucked me, there was nothing else but me and him, the sweet pain he poured inside of me, and the promise of the rapturing pleasure he never failed to keep.

"Tell me you didn't leave me for another guy." He said as he thrust inside me. "Tell me you didn't lie to me when you said *me too*."

"Laius…"

"Tell me, Jo, because I'm losing my fucking mind here."

I moaned loudly. "Laius, please."

"Tell me I didn't fall in love with another bitch that fucked me over and shit all over my life."

A gasp stuck in my throat. Did he just say he loved me? Out loud? In this fucked up way, at this fucked up time of all times?

He pulled my hair, my real hair, and I became aware I wasn't wearing my wig. I blinked to realize I didn't have my contacts on either. He must have taken them both off. He fucked me harder. His length was splitting me in half more painfully than pleasurably. "Speak, Jo. Did you fuck him?"

"No. Goddammit, Laius. He said he was going to kill you. He took my gun, and he threatened to kill you if I didn't break up with you and be with him. I did what I had to do to protect you."

He stilled. Then the next instant his arms were holding me as he rubbed his face on my back and then kissed me hard on my cheek. "You silly girl. You think you needed to protect me from a little boy?"

"You don't know him. He's sick, and he would have done it."

"You should have told me."

"I couldn't risk getting you hurt in any way because I love you, too, Furore. I love you so much Laius Lazzarini."

He pulled my hair again, this time to bring my lips into his, and he devoured me in a heated passionate kiss, slamming into me hard and fast, until I was screaming into his mouth, the orgasm so intense my whole body was shuddering. He followed right away, filling me with the warm gushes of his seed.

He pulled his mouth away from me to allow us both to breathe, but his gaze and arms never left me. We stayed like this for a while, wrapped around each other, with him inside me, our eyes doing all the talking. Then he kissed me again. "You have to tell me exactly what happened and the name of that boy so I could take care of things, so *I* could keep *you* safe."

I told him everything but left out three pieces of information. My ex's name. The fact the he raped me with a gun. And why I was on my way to Chicago.

Michele. I was calling him when Furore's men attacked me. Shit, did my call go through? "Where is my phone? Did your men get my phone?"

"Who the fuck cares? I'll get you another one. They're fine, by the way. Hook who you shot, and Texas who you almost broke his legs with your kicks. Where did you learn these moves and who taught you how to shoot?"

I huffed. "Whom."

"What?"

"Hook *whom* you shot, and Texas *whom* you almost broke his legs."

He pulled out of me, his cum spilling between my thighs. "You're giving me a grammar lesson right now?"

"I'm sorry they were hurt, but your men were *kidnapping* me. I didn't know who they were. And those moves didn't do me any good. They still succeeded at abducting me."

He unchained me, and I let out a sigh of relief. Those things hurt. I tried to sit, but every muscle and limb of mine was sore. Then the searing pain in the flesh of my buttock infuriated me. "I can't believe you gave me a property tattoo." I was officially a biker's slut. How did my life turn that way? From a high school English teacher to a patch whore with a property tattoo?

You were a teacher who slept with her students. A patch whore isn't so much of a downgrade from a teacher slut.

"I can't believe you're still dodgy about all the shit that happened. I need straight answers, Jo, starting with the name of that punk."

"Why? So you'd kill him? How does that make you any different from him, Laius?"

"I told you never to compare me to another guy."

"Well, you two are oddly alike, and I sure know how to pick them."

"Jo! He pulled a motherfucking gun at you!"

"Because he's jealous and overtly possessive just like you. He saw me with you, so he decided to take me back whatever it took. How was that any different from your kidnapping me when you thought I left with another guy? How was he threatening to kill you any different from you threatening to kill him now?" How was cuffing me to a bed and fucking me to reclaim me any different from what Tirone did to me in my apartment? Yes, Tirone was more extreme with his methods, but the principles were still the same.

How did I fall for the same dark and twisted type twice? How was I turned on by all that toxicity and violence? How did I feel safe amidst all that danger? Because, fuck me, I was glad Laius did what he did and I was with him, under his protection.

"Are you saying that I'm sick, too?" he asked.

What if he was? What if he wasn't just a criminal, resorting to violence to solve problems because it was the only way he was accustomed to? What if Tirone wasn't sick at all and was just evil like his father or decided to follow his dad's lead? I didn't know anything anymore. I was more than confused and my moral compass wasn't pointing north anymore because there was one thing I knew for sure.

Despite all that had happened, all the pain and heartache and rage it caused me, I was madly in love with Furore, and deep down, I didn't exactly hate Tirone.

Laius bent, meeting my gaze, his an equal amount of menace and fury. "I don't care what you call me. Fuck, I don't even care if you hate me. You'll never leave me again or be with another guy until the day you die. You're mine, Jo, and you'll fucking stay that way forever."

I didn't know if I should run for the hills or bow at his feet and beg him to take me and let me drown in everything he had to give me no matter how dark it was going to get.

He tipped my chin up with his finger. "Give me the name of your shitty ex so I can get it over with."

"He's a kid, Laius."

"Not anymore."

"I will if you promise me you won't kill him. Scare him away but don't kill him." He probably wouldn't hurt him anyway. Tirone was one of them, or, at least, the son of one. MC people valued their brotherhood more than anything.

"The name, Jo."

I'd have to tell him sooner or later since I'd become a part of the Night Skulls. The tattoo on my ass made it so. But why could he not just promise me he wouldn't end Tirone's life?

I couldn't be responsible for that. If I could, I'd have killed him myself or told Michele to do it.

Michele. What if my call went through and he heard what happened and figured I was kidnapped? He'd look for me and if he found out Laius did it, shit would hit the fan. Fuck.

A knock on the door stopped my unhinged train of thoughts.

"The fuck! I said no one interrupts me!" Laius shouted.

"It's important, Prez. Cover your ass 'cause I gotta come in."

He jabbed a finger at me. "We're not done." He gathered my panties and jeans off the hardwood floor and threw them at me. Then he pulled his own jeans up and zipped it.

I covered myself, taking notice of the room. My wig was on a chair in a corner. My contact case on the nightstand. Every piece of furniture in the room was black. Red wallpaper everywhere. Riding gear scattered on the floor, the tiny dresser and poked out of a wardrobe. Tattoo equipment was still on the bed. There was a door on the left which I assumed was the bathroom door.

"Where's my purse?" I fastened the hook of the wig and combed the hair with my fingers. "The solution for my contacts is in it."

"No time." He gave me a pair of pilot sunglasses. "Put these on."

I did as he opened the door. Fort came in, a shit eating grin on his face. "Howdy, doll. Had a nice nap?"

"What's so fucking important?" Laius fumed.

Fort nodded his head to the side. "Guess who just pulled up by the gates?"

"I don't have time for games, Fort. Spit it out."

"Rex."

My head jerked toward them, and Laius's lips were curving on the corner with a smile. I smiled, too, happy for him. Finally, his prodigal son returned.

"Get him in. I'll be right out." Laius shut the door behind Fort and pulled me into a bear hug. "I love you. This wouldn't have happened without you."

"What did I do?"

"The letter. When I went to give it to him, he wasn't home. His mother took it from me, and I lost all hope. I thought she'd never give it to him, but then after I found out you were gone, I headed back to Rosewood to get my shit and send my men after you. There, I found this." He pulled a piece of paper out of his pocket and gave it to me. "He wrote me back."

"That's amazing." I took the letter. "You should go. Be the first to receive him."

"You wait here, okay. I'll get him settled in, and then I'll introduce you."

"Wait, you told him about me?"

"I called him this morning after the brothers brought you home. I thought it'd be better that way, to be upfront about us so he'd know beforehand what awaited him here."

"Okay. What did he say?"

"He said he was old enough to know I wasn't keeping my dick in my pants all those years, and he was okay with it. Then he told me, when I was done with you, to give you to him so he could show you what a good dicking was really like."

My jaw dropped. "What the… When you told me he wasn't very nice, you weren't exaggerating."

He laughed. "It's just a joke. That's how I knew he was okay with it for real. And he's here, Jo. He really is here, thanks to you."

"I'm so happy for you, Laius."

"Wait here. I'll be right back."

"Sure. Just go."

He kissed me and dashed away. I was so
happy for him. Finally, we were receiving
some good news. Sitting on the edge of the
bed, I unfolded the paper and started reading.

I know you all, and will a while uphold
The unyoked humour of your idleness.
Yet herein will I imitate the sun,
Who doth permit the base contagious clouds
To smother up his beauty from the world,
That when he please again to be himself,
Being wanted he may be more wondered at
By breaking through the foul and ugly mists
Of vapours that did seem to strangle him.
If all the year were playing holidays,
To sport would be as tedious as to work;
But when they seldom come, they wished-for come,
And nothing pleaseth but rare accidents.
So when this loose behaviour I throw off
And pay the debt I never promised,
By how much better than my word I am,
By so much shall I falsify men's hopes;
And like bright metal on a sullen ground,
My reformation, glitt'ring o'er my fault,
Shall show more goodly and attract more eyes
Than that which hath no foil to set it off.
I'll so offend to make offence a skill,
Redeeming time when men think least I will.

I frowned at the lines, my heart thudding
with every word. This was Prince Hal's

soliloquy from Henry IV. This was not by any means encouraging or words written by a son ready to give his father a chance. It was ominous to say the least, if it wasn't all alarming.

But the threat that lied between the lines wasn't what caused the palpitations of my heart. It was the handwriting.

I wiped my forehead and pulled up the sunglasses to read clearly, hoping it wasn't my mind tricking me.

I received your letter, and I accept. I'm coming to Texas tomorrow.

Tirone.

A wild gasp burst out of me at the same time I heard a voice coming from outside the door. Tirone Wisely's voice. Tirone fucking Lazzarini.

All the blood rushing out of my body, my head a big cloud of dizziness, I fell off the bed face down.

The door burst open. Then Laius was standing over. "Jo!" His arms carried me, and then my back was lying against something soft. "What happened?"

I could barely open my eyes, but I saw him. It was really him standing at the door. Tirone. My Tirone was Laius's son.

"Baby, answer me. Dammit. Someone get me some water!" Laius yelled.

"I...I..." I pointed at the door, seeing double, Tirone's face—faces—coming toward me. Words I couldn't bring myself to say shivered on my mouth.

Tirone sat next me on the bed and opened a bottle of water from his messenger bag. He held my head and made me drink, smirking at me. "Here."

I gulped, staring at him.

"Rex, this is—"

"Miss Meneceo," Tirone finished Laius's sentence, and my heart dropped to my feet.

Laius scowled at us. "Do you know each other?"

This was it. This was how we all died in a fit of rage.

Fort barged in out of nowhere. I'd recognize that human tank even if I were dead, not just on the verge of passing out. "Prez, get her outta here. We have another visitor."

"Fuck. Who?"

"Lanza."

"Armando?"

Fort shook his head. "Enzio Lanza himself."

I was wrong. I wasn't going to die because I fell in love with my ex-boyfriend's deadly jealous dad while his son was even worse in that department. I wasn't going to die in a fit of rage between two possessive men after I ditched one in the worst way ever and drugged the other and abandoned him on the road or the revenge that was bound to come after.

I was going to die in a Mafia war.

Enzio Lanza was the boss of the Lanza Mafia family, and my blood was the key to the new kingdom he thirsted after.

He'd found me and just arrived to collect my soul.

And when Furore discovered my ex was his son, would he still be my protector or the one who delivered me to the devils that wanted me dead?

FURORE

To be continued…
*****

Thanks for Reading, Playlist and Part Two!

I hope you've enjoyed the beginning of Jo, Furore and Tirone's story. As you know, this is a duet which means there are many questions and conflicts yet to be resolved in book 2. Like how did Ty and Jo hook up? How was their relationship like? How did Michele become Jo's papa? What's really wrong with Ty? And so many more. There are so many secrets left to unravel and conflicts to resolve in the next book. Tirone, part two and the double in size conclusion of this duet is ready for you to devour.

Read Tirone now

https://books2read.com/tirone

If you haven't read Forbidden Cruel Italians Mafia series and anxious to know who the Lanzas and the Bellomo are, this is for you:

- **Start The Italians series PREQUEL FREE with The Cruel Italian**
  https://bookhip.com/KFJQQCM
- **For Enzio Lanza's book,** read and download The Italian Marriage now
- **For Tino Bellomo's book,** read **The Italian Obsession**
- **For Dom Lanza's book,** download The Italian Dom
- **For Leo Bellomo's book download The Italian Son**

To take a break from dark reads but still get the spice of hot Italian men:
- **Read Mike Gennaro's book** The Italian Heartthrob
- **Read Fabio Zappa's book** The Italian Happy Ever After

Join my Newsletter for extra scenes, free books and updates
Njadelbooks.com

SOUNDTRACK

Just Like Heaven by The Lumineers

Numb To Everything by Citizen Soldier

Only Happy when It Rains by Sam Tinnesz
and Holy Wars

Jumpsuit by Twenty One Pilots

Love Me or Leave Me by Munn

Shakes by Stevie Howie

Looks Like Me by Dean Lewis

Petrichor by Cassyette

Listen to the full playlist on Spotify
https://spoti.fi/3PcYCI2

ALSO BY N.J. ADEL

Contemporary Romance
The Italian Heartthrob
The Italian Happy Ever After
The Italian Marriage
The Italian Obsession
The Italian Dom
The Italian Son

Paranormal Reverse Harem
All the Teacher's Pet Beasts
All the Teacher's Little Belles
All the Teacher's Bad Boys
All the Teacher's Prisoners

Reverse Harem Erotic Romance
Her Royal Harem: Complete Box Set

Dark MC and Mafia Romance
I Hate You then I Love You Collection
Furore
Tirone
Dusty
Cameron

AUTHOR BIO

N. J. Adel, the author of All the Teacher's Pets, The Italians, and The Night Skulls MC series, is a cross genre author. From chocolate to books and book boyfriends, she likes it DARK and SPICY.

Bikers, rock stars, dirty Hollywood heartthrobs, smexy guards and men who serve. She loves it all.

She is a loather of cats and thinks they are Satan's pets. She used to teach English by day and write fun smut by night with her German Shepherd, Leo. Now, she only writes the fun smut.